MY DIRTY GAME

by

Timothy Fakorede O.

This book is a work of a fiction and drama, any resemblance with anyone, either living or dead, is a pure coincidence with the author's imagination.

Gosh! It was almost 7:30am. I rushed out of the bedroom, picked up a kettle, performed ablution and prayed to the God. Only God knows if the prayer was even answered or not because I could not concentrate on it. I rushed from there to the bathroom; I took my bath, brushed my teeth and dressed up for work. I marched out like a soldier going for war. I got to the street where I could get a bus to my place of work very fast but it was quiet unfortunate that I could not't get a bus on time and it was around 8:30am. I started murmuring when I saw a bus coming. "Station road", I said to the driver "come", the driver replied, is four dollars sir. The driver said and I frowned at him, but did not alter a word. I got to where to drop, gave him four dollar and alighted peacefully. I trekked a little bit and got to the office. It was already 8:50am.

"You are a bit late today", said Mrs. Hillary. "Yes ma". I replied.

It was not less than a minute that I took my sit when Mrs. Mary entered and greeted everyone on seat and came directly to me. She was one of my bosses at the office before she was been posted to another department. "You will see an alert very soon. Grandma is coming for clinic today and the money will be needed to take care of her". She said. "Ok ma". I replied. That was not the first time of cashing fund through my Bank account. It was so, because his uncle that does send the money could only locate that bank around him. After two minutes when she had left, I heard a message sound on my phone. I picked it and checked the message. Hiss! It was an unsolicited text message from my service provider. I hissed and threw the phone on the table with anger.

"Kyle, please come", said Mr. Robert. He was also one of my bosses like Mrs. Mary. He counted eighty thousand dollars and handed it to me, with a paper that had an account number, account name and the name of the bank. "Drop it into that Bank account", he said. "Alright sir", I replied.

Since Oxford Bank is not too far from Global bank I was sent to initially, I decided to take my ATM card along incase the money drop into my account. I checked my wallet for the card but could not find it. I searched my bag and everywhere I thought of, but I could not find it. I decided to zoom off to the Oxford bank. On my way to the bank, I started tasking my brain where I put the card and the answer appeared to me as if I am a BBC news-caster who reads on the screen. Oh, yah! It was in the pocket of a pair trouser I hung in my wardrobe. I smiled. I continued with the trek when I heard a deep voice from my back

I looked at the back and it was a huge dark guy with tinted hair.

"Chairman, could you show me the way to Wilfred Restaurant"? He asked me. "Just go straight by your left and ask when you get to the next junction", I replied. I left the spot and moved to Oxford bank. On getting there, I picked up a deposit slip and dug my right hand in my pocket to obtain my pen and the fund in order to fill the denomination as arranged in the slip. Where did I put it now? I searched my pockets thoroughly but could not see the money given to me. I started sweating despite the fact that the air conditioners were on. My mind was seriously disturbed and the heart started pounding like a locomotive machine. What could have happened? Has the guy I answered taken the money from me? I was lost on this thought when I heard my phone ringing. I looked at the screen and it was Mr Stephen. Should I pick it or neglect it? What would I tell him if I pick it? Did I even know why he is calling? I started asking myself those rhetorical questions while I lost the first call. It started ringing again; I summoned courage to pick it. "Hel hel hel". I started stammering while he took up from me. "Hello Kyle". You have left the money in the office. Why? He lamented. I could not belief what I've just heard and I nearly told him to recap. "I've been looking for it here sir". I replied with grateful heart and quickly left the bank for office; I collected the money and got back to the bank within a blink of an eye. I entered the details and joined the queue.

It remained only four persons before me when my phone beeped. I neglected the message thinking it was the same usual unsolicited text message from 5052 again. After some seconds, my phone started ringing. I looked at the screen and it was Mrs. Mary. I picked the call. "Hello Kyle, where are you". She asked. "Oxford bank ma", I replied. "Have you seen the alert?" I was called just now that the money has been sent into your account, she said. "Yes ma", I replied. "Would you cash it while coming back to office?" She asked. "Definitely," I replied.

Then, it was my turn. I gave the money and slip to the cashier, to perform his professional duty, he did so and returned a copy of the slip to me. "Thank you for banking with us". He said and I left the queue.

I took out my phone to confirm what Mrs Mary said and it was true. I need to go back home for my ATM card. I said to myself and I rushed out of the bank. On a normal occasion, it will take me like fifteen minutes to reach St. David High School where I normally drop before trekking to my final destination and since I had no alternative, I stopped a cab. "St. David", I said. "Enter. It's four dollars". He said. "No problem", I replied.

Some kilometers to the St. David, we ran into a stupid hold-up which got me annoyed. I felt like dropping from the bus and continued with my legs. While thinking of that, I heard the sound of siren of a Black Maria from the back and before I knew it, the way was freed and that gave my cab the chance of taking me to the St. David quickly. This is a public high School with fence and two gates at the entrance, but since the fence had collapsed at the back, it has created avenue for people's passage. But I ran out of luck on this very day just because when I alighted from the cab, I discovered that the gate had been padlocked due to some reasons unknown to me. I need to cover a great distance through another route before I could reach home. I said to myself and I did not't know when I picked a race. I got home within a short period of time. "Hope no problem?" My sister asked curiously. "No ma". I came for my ATM, I explained. "Alright", she said. I went directly to where I put the trouser, took out both ATM and School ID card and put them in my back pocket and rushed out again. It was around quarter to two. I took another race back to the street where to get a cab but decided not to take bus. I took bike instead. Thank God I did not take bus, because there was another hectic traffic jam but my bike scaled through easily. I was fortunate when I got to Global bank because people were very scanty at the ATM machine stand and there was another free machine. I went straight to it, took out my ATM card and inserted it. I was waiting for it to be ready so as to input my pin but all I could get on the screen was "hardware error" and the card was rejected...

I took the card, cleaned it and made another trial, but the problem persisted. I wanted to go to customer care immediately but a thought came over me to try another machine, which of course I did. "Usage App Error" was the new message I got from another machine I used. Since I have satisfied my conscience, then I decided to go the customer care. I left the ATM stand and went directly into the bank. I thought I was in a market because everywhere was just jam-packed. Though, those that wanted to withdraw and those that wanted to deposit were on a long zigzag queue but the story was not the same with those at the customer care section, it was just like the movement of gaseous particles in a container colliding with one another and with the wall of the container that occurs in a chemical reaction, and since there was no order at the place, I had the opportunity of tendering my case to an attendant. "Ma, I was trying to withdraw through the ATM machine but was not successful", I complained.

"What was the message you got from the machine?" She asked.

"Usage App Error", I replied.

"Your English is not correct", she said.

"What an embarrassment! How do you mean?" I responded furiously.

"I did not mean to rude to you but only trying to explain to you that the machine could not give out such message. So, you will need to recheck so as to know the problem to work on", she explained.

I raised above the taunt and remained unruffled. I went back to the ATM stand, inserted the card. The same message appeared on the screen and I snapped the information with my phone as evidence. I went back to her and showed her. She started looking at the message like a primary four student given WAEC question to solve. After some minutes, she asked me to write a report which I did with tick and gave it to her. She dragged the keyboard of the system on the table towards her and checked my account details. She looked at my face, and then faced one of her colleagues. "Charles, what could make machine write this while the account is not fixed?" she showed him my report. So, you did not have the knowledge? No wonder you claimed the English was not correct I nearly said when Charles gave response to her question.

"It has damaged". He said."

What could have damaged this neat card?" I asked.

"Maybe you packed it with a phone", he replied.

"I have never put the two together because I know the implication", I responded.

The guy refused to say anything again and started punching the keyboard of the computer in front of him. Look at this stupid boy using me to press keyboard I almost said when I heard my phone ringing. It was Mrs. Mary. I picked it up and explained the situation on ground to her and dropped the call. I could not tolerate the guy's ego, so I decided to go and face my first attendant. "Ma, what is the next line of action to seek redress?" I asked.

"You will need to apply for another ATM and hundred dollars will be charged from your account". She replied.

I stood at akimbo thinking of the next line of action to take when my phone started ringing again. I looked at the screen and it was her again, Mrs. Mary. I picked it up and I was about to say 'hello' when someone held my hand from the back...

I turned my head to know who was holding me and it was a security agent. "did not you see the notice that receiving calls is prohibited in the bank!" he yelled at me.

I was shocked and dropped the call unknowingly.

"Am sorry sir", I apologized.

I went back to the first attendant.

"Ma, would I be able to get the ATM today if I apply?" I asked.

"ATM form is not available for now, you will need to come as early as possible tomorrow morning", she replied.

"But the money is needed right now in the hospital to take care of an unhealthy patient", I tried to explain to her.

"Perhaps, you withdraw through counter then, that is the only option you are left with", she advised.

I looked at the situation on ground; the queue was still as long as river Nile.

"I could not come out of this queue if I join", I said to myself.

"Ma, what favour could you offer me if at all I want to withdraw through counter?" I asked her.

"Don't worry! You will only be charged of two hundred and fifty naira from your account", she said.

"Am ok with it provided that I will get the money", I responded.

"Go to that lady at the extreme end and request for withdrawal slip", she pointed to a fair lady, very beautiful and portable in size. She should be an I.T student like me, I guessed.

"Well done", I greeted her.

"How may I help you?", she asked.

"I need a withdrawal slip", I replied.

"Do you have your ID card with you?", she asked.

"Yes, is with me", I replied.

(She detached a slip and filled it.)

"Where is your ID card", she asked.

(I gave out my school ID card to her).

She looked at my face and smiled. Why is she smiling at me? Are we from the same school or she has developed interest in me? I was lost in those thoughts when I heard from her. "Sir, I don't mean your school ID card, but National ID card or better still, Your driving license", she explained.

"But you said ID card and besides, what is wrong with my school ID card?", I asked.

"Am sorry sir, we don't recognize school ID card. In the light of this, I will only give you this slip, but you can't withdraw with it", she said and handed the slip to me.

"What should I use it for since I could not use it to withdraw?" I asked in pity.

"It's yours, since I have detached it and your names had been written on it", she replied.

I felt disturbed and started thinking of the next action to take and that was when I remembered that my PVC (Permanent Voters Card) could be of use as a substitute to National ID card.

It was already 3:15pm. I left the bank for office in hurry so as to take my PVC and come back before the bank close for the day.

I branched at Mrs. Mary's office and told her what I had gone through.

She looked at me with pity and showed her sympathy.

"Am very sorry for letting you experienced such turmoil. Perhaps you delay it till tomorrow", she said in a pitiable mood.

"No ma. Let me take my PVC at the office and give it the last trial for today", I replied and left for office.

"Are you just coming from the bank?", Mrs.Hillary questioned.

"Yes ma", I replied.

"That's serious!" she exclaimed.

I started checking where I put my PVC, but could not find it. Another problem! It should be at home too, I thought.

"I will be back ma", I said to my boss.

"Are you still going back to the bank?" she asked.

"Yes ma", I replied and I left. She uttered a statement but I did not care to listen.

I checked Mrs.Mary in her office and explained to her that I could not't see the PVC but I have prepared for the worst.

"How do you want to go about it?" she asked.

"I have decided to go and meet the manager", I replied.

"Do you think they will allow you to see him", she asked with confusion.

"Don't worry ma, I will", I replied optimistically.

"Alright dear, thanks so much", she said and I zoomed off back to the bank.

On getting to the bank, I changed my thought of meeting the manager, so, I went back to the first attendant.

"Ma, I presented my school ID card to her for the slip, but she insisted that I must present my National ID card", I lamented.

She looked at me with pity and collected the slip from me.

"Where did you open your account?" she asked.

"New York, United State", I replied.

She signed it and gave it to me.

"You are good to collect the money on the counter", she said.

I was a little bit relieved.

"Thanks for your support ma, but I thought you are helping me to withdraw the money", I said.

"As a good Citizen, you have to join the queue, and besides, you know am on duty and customers could be here at any time. Sequel to that, I can't leave my seat", she continued, "am sorry incase I have disappointed you", she concluded.

On hearing that, I became hopeless like an orphan who lost her parents due to war and still lost in a desert. My heart vibrated and my eyes were filled with tears. Who would come to my rescue? I was lost in my thought when I heard from her.

"Bro, try to understand me. It's not that I am being wicked at you or maybe if you could go to that man", she pointed to a security agent, "If he could be of help", she advised.

I bought her idea and went to him. I tried to explain to him.

"Who asked you to come to me? Am begging, we don't assist to withdraw and why can't she withdraw for you too?" he said in anger.

So, I'm now a basket ball throwing up and down. No problem! I said and went back to the lady.

"It's high time I left for office. I can't join this queue. Probably I'll come back tomorrow if and only if the patient sustain the condition till tomorrow, but hope my account will not be charged for this slip?" I asked.

"You have to return it so as not to be charged", she replied.

I gave it to her and she crossed it.

I went back to office and told Mrs.Mary the latest development.

"I have told grandma to delay the check up till tomorrow since we could not get the money today, so how shall we go about it tomorrow?" she asked.

"I have decided to go directly from the house to the bank tomorrow morning", I explained.

"Are you cashing it through counter or how?" she curiously asked.

"I prefer applying for ATM, but if cashing it through counter would be the faster, I will use that", I replied.

"Alright, let me follow you to take permission from Boss that, you may likely come late tomorrow", she said.

It was 3:45pm that day and of which my closing time used to be 3:00pm, and since the permission had been granted, then I left office for home.

FOLLOWING DAY

I got up from bed by Mrs. Mary's call telling me on phone that grandma was in a critical condition and needed urgent medical attention. In that case, the money will be needed to cater for her treatment.

I left home as early as possible so as to get the money probably through counter, but it was quiet unfortunate that I still met people on queue. I got confused to the extent of contemplating whether to withdraw through counter by queuing or apply for the ATM. But, since ATM will still be useful for me in the nearest future, then I decided to apply for it.

I informed the first customer attendant that attended to me in the previous day and she instructed me to go into a room so as to get a form. I left for the room and felt like saying I was no longer interested when I saw many a customer to be attended to, but I summoned courage and collected the form, filled it and joined the queue for ATM.

While on the queue, my phone started ringing, I looked at the screen and it was Mrs. Mary, but I decided not to pick it. She continued calling and since the call was disturbing, I decided to put the phone on vibration.

After some minutes, it became my turn and could not just belief it, the attendant was that fair lady that refused to sign for me in the previous day. She smiled and stared at me when she saw me.

"Good morning gentleman", she greeted me.

"I pray this morning is good", I replied jokingly.

"It will surely good", she responded.

I submitted my form to her with the PVC.

"Where is your school ID card", she asked and winked me.

"But, you said you don't welcome my school ID card yesterday, why asking for it now?" I asked. (Though, I gave her.)

"That unit is different from this one. Your school ID card is needed here", she explained in a seductive manner.

"You will have to do the photocopy of these cards", she said.

"Where could I do it?" I asked.

"Give it to that security man at the door to do it for you", she said pointing to a man.

She gave me my PVC and the school ID card, and then I took them to the man as instructed.

"Why did you not give it to me when others were giving me", he complained.

"I was not aware about it", I said.

He murmured for some minutes and collected only the PVC from me.

"But, sir, you are to do the two cards for me", I said.

"You need the PVC only", he yelled at me.

Then, I kept mute. He left and came back after some minutes with the photocopy.

Then, my phone started ringing, it was a strange number and I ignored it. I looked at the time, it was after twelve, and then I rushed back to the lady.

"Here is the photocopy", I tendered it to her.

"Where is the second one?" she asked.

"He did only one for me saying the second one is not needed", I replied.

"Who is in control? I said I need the two. Go back to him and tell him that I said he should do it before I get back to him", she said furiously.

See me see trouble, see the way this small rat is sending me up and down. No problem! I said to myself.

I went back to the security, pleaded to him and he did it for me quickly, I now went back to her. She issued me another ATM card.

"Go back to the attendant that attended to you yesterday and give the card to her", she instructed.

I quickly went to her handed the card to her. My phone started vibrating, I looked at the screen and it was Matt, my co. IT student, but she has completed her own training. I neglected the call. By then, the attendant was ready

"Take it back inside to change your pin", she said.

"What's all this?" I murmured and collected the card from her.

I went back to the fair lady.

"I was directed to bring this card back to you", I said.

"Not here, but to that madam receiving call", she pointed to a fat woman. While rushing to her, I saw her standing. "I will be back shortly, my attention is needed by the MD",she told her colleagues and rushed out.

I looked at the time and it was 12:45pm, I felt like crying. If I had known, I would not have applied for this. I started blaming myself. The phone started vibrating again, but I did not even bother to check who was calling because I was moody.

After ten minutes, the woman came back to her seat and the following conversation transpired;

Madam; where is your card?

Me; this is it ma (I gave it to her)

Madam; are you a student?

Me; yes ma.

Madam; where is your school ID card?

Me; this is it ma (I gave it to her)

Madam; I can't accept this card from you because it has expired.

Me; not yet expired ma. My school is still on session and since am still on I.T; the new I.D card could not be issued for now.

Madam; it's not possible! Never!

Me; I am an IT student now.

Madam; Amanda, come (she called the fair lady, and that was when I knew her name) check this card, look at the session, 2010/2011 and we are in 2012.

Amanda; the card is valid ma. It seemed they were delayed by strike.

Madam; I still can't accept this from him unless he proves his studentship.

Me; what else do you still need when I have told you am still exercising my I.T (I yelled at her and walked out on her to where customer's wardrobe was, took my logbook with my and other relevant credentials, I went back to show her; she checked it very well and became sober)

Madam; enter your pin on the machine.

Me; (I entered my four digit number) what next?

Madam: your card is ready for use.

I collected the card and looked back nostalgically to where the journey started from. I packed my belongings on her table and left for the ATM stand to withdraw.

I was fortunate to see a free machine and quickly inserted my new card without any delay. I kept on looking at the screen waiting for it to be ready so as to enter my pin when I saw "please, insert your card". I could not trust my eyes with what I saw, so I wiped my face with my palm and re-checked.

"Please, insert your card" was still on the screen.

"Which card again, what about the one I've inserted?" I kept on asking the machine as if it was a human being.

"You should not have used the machine, it has swallowed someone's card before now", a lady said to me.

I checked the time and it was 1:15pm. I was so furious and went back to the first attendant.

"You are still here!" she asked in surprise.

"In fact, am even fed up with this your bank. Could you belief that, my newly collected card has been swallowed by a machine", I lamented.

"Go to the room where the card was issued and ask of Dallas", she said.

I marched in like a soldier.

"Am looking for Dallas?" I asked a staff standing not knowing that he was the one I was looking for.

"Any problem?" he asked.

"There is!" I took my time to explain to him. He was about to speak when a short woman like a mortar spoke for him, "you will have to come back because he just left the place now and you can't ask him to go back there again", she lamented.

I went crimson immediately.

"What are you telling me? What was he employed for? I could not hear you, could you recap?" lamenting continued, "I've been parading here since yesterday and the card was just issued some minutes ago and your useless machine swallowed it, and you are still telling me to come back later", I said, "You must be joking", I poured angrily.

Yes! Good! I like you! Well done! The customers around hailed me and the woman started shivering like water lily.

"I will get it for you, just take it easy", Dallas said in a low voice.

He was about to leave when a woman with the same problem as mine came in.

"Stay here while I check for both of you", said Dallas.

We both stood at the entrance of the room like a security agent.

He came back after some minutes (sweating).

"Who is Peter Kate Jones?" he asked.

"Am the one", the woman responded.

He handed an ATM card to her.

"Uncle, which machine did you use?" He asked with tremble in his voice.

"We used the same machine", I responded.

"Sir, I guess the system has returned your card, because I could not see it. Therefore, you will need to go back outside before it is being taken", he said.

On hearing this, my eyes bulged out like that of dragon-fly thirsty of water and I fled out of the bank to the ATM stand where I met a guy standing beside the machine that swallowed my card.

"Chairman, please, did you help me see a card?" I asked like a beggar looking for a Samaritan.

"What is your name sir?" he asked.

"Bradley Kyle James", I replied.

He handed my card to me and went to sit in a Toyota Camry car.

I tried another system with the card and it was successful.

At last! I went to thank the guy who kept my card for me, and that was when I got to know that he was a son of Mrs. Peter. No wonder he stood at the ATM!

I left for office after the appreciation.

On getting to office, I checked Mrs. Mary in her office but she was not around, then, I decided to send "call me back" to her and to the rest of the numbers I've missed intentionally. Then, I left for my office. After some minutes, my phone started vibrating, an unknown number, then I picked it up.

"Hello, Kyle, where have you put your phone since?" (It was Mrs. Mary's voice.)

"It was not with me ma. I'm now available ma, I've even checked on you in your office", I replied.

"I'm with grandma. I'll join you soon" she said.

She came around after some minutes.

"You almost turned me to something else when you did not pick the calls up. My mind was not at rest and I have even come to the bank to check on you but I could not see you. I've been dodging boss since morning, because I did not know what to tell him if he asked about you", she said

"I'm sorry ma, I left my phone in the bag and kept it in the wardrobe outside, so I did not know it was ringing until when I went to take my logbook and saw the missed calls", I lied.

She thanked and appreciated me for the great job I have done for her and she tried to compensate me with token, but I rejected it in the first instance and later collected it from her when the frustration was too much.

I took permission at office and went back home after some minutes because I was seriously tired.

I got home around 3:00pm, ate the food prepared for me by my sister, then headed to the bathroom to take my bath and slept off soon after my bath.

I woke up around 8:15pm, picked up my phone and saw six missed calls from an unknown number. Since I had no airtime on my mobile phone, I decided to send "call me back" to the number.

After some minutes, a message entered and when I checked it, it contained the pin of a recharge card from the unknown number, I recharged the card immediately.

Wow! Who could have sent me this worthful recharge card!! I was flabbergasted and decided to call the number straight-away. I was about to dial the number when my phone started vibrating. It was another unknown number and picked it up without any hesitation.

"Hello, please who is this?" I asked inquisitively.

"It's me; you can't even recognize my voice on phone again!" (It was a lovely voice of a lady which sounded familiar) she said silkily.

"Is this not Louisa's voice?" I asked doubtfully.

"Yes!" she replied joyfully and giggled

Me: Wow! Can't just belief this! Where did you get my number?

Louisa: don't worry about that . I learnt that you are in New York city.

Me: yeah. Who told you? (I asked curiously)

Louisa: we shall talk when we see on Saturday. I've seriously missed you.

Me: really? Same here too. Are you also in New York city?

Louisa: no, but I will fall in on Saturday.

Me: no problem. But wait! Were you the one who sent me airtime some minutes ago?

Louisa: me! No, or should I send you?

Me: don't bother.

Louisa: catch up with you on Saturday dear.

Me: alright. I wish you Journey mercy in advance.

Louisa: thanks dear. Bye! (She ended the call).

I can't just belief I could still hear from Louisa (I was overwhelmed with the memory we shared together when we were in school) I was lost in the emotional feeling when I remembered that I have not called the number that sent me the airtime. Then, I dialed the number...

"hello, please, who am I on to?"

"it's me, Amanda" she replied. (It was another lovely voice from a lady)

"did you mean Amanda, the basketball player?" I asked jokingly

"no!" she replied stressing and giggled.

"Then, which Amanda?" I asked with seriousness.

"From the bank you are banking with", she said in a silky tone.

Me: oh yah! How did you get my number?

Amanda: from your form now, or you have forgotten that I was the one who entered your details into the system?

Me: What a clever game! No wonder they employed you.

Amanda: stop teasing.

Me: I am not, but only saying the fact.

Amanda: Ok Thanks anyway.

Me: so, you were the one who sent me the card?

Amanda: don't mind me. I did when I discovered you were out of airtime. It's just a token and I hope you have accepted it the way it was?

Me: I can't just belief this! So, your type still exists on earth? Thanks so much. You are highly appreciated.

Amanda: the pleasure is mine.

Me: I guess you have information to pass across to me.

Amanda: not really, but just to apologize for what our organization made you pass through. I decided to do this on their behalf.

Me: baby, you are so kind! Are you truly a human being? Because, I've not come across someone like you. Everything about you is just perfect.

Amanda: Really!

Me: I mean it baby. Sequel to what you apologized for, it was nothing, but only a challenge which has added to my boldness and rigidity.

Amanda: I could notice that while reacting in our office. I so much cherished and saluted your courage and boldness. I was really impressed. In fact, you are such a man!

Me: are you trying to kid me?

Amanda: I'm seriously not kidding you. I mean it. Keep it up.

Me: thanks so much for the compliment.

Amanda: hope you have granted the apology?

Me: even, more than granted.

Amanda: how will I be sure you have granted it?

Me: I swear to God, I have granted it.

Amanda: Ok But if I invite you to my place, would you honour my invitation?

Me: that will be awesome! I will definitely do.

Amanda: you mean it!

Me: of course, yes.

Amanda: I'm now inviting you to my haven on Sunday.

Me: that's serious! I thought you were joking.

Amanda: joking? I'm not.

Me: by what time then?

Amanda: I want you to choose any convenient time of your own since am going nowhere on that day.

Me: let's make it 4:00pm then.

Amanda: that's too far now. I will be bored at home. Could you make it 12noon at least?

Me: no problem. I will give it a trial.

Amanda: thanks so much dear.

Me: the pleasure is mine. Let me have the address.

Amanda: don't worry, I'll send you the address via text message.

Me: alright.

Amanda: thanks so much for making my night a colourful one.

Me: the pleasure is mine. Take care of yourself and do have a splendid night rest.

Amanda: and you too.

Me: yeah. Good night. (I hung up the call)

What has just happened now? Amanda! From the bank! Am I dreaming? Then, I started picturing the scenarios that happened in the bank and her stances towards me. Has this lady felt in love with me? Love at the first sight, can it be possible? In the course of thinking, my heart lighted up and my face was full of smile...

I stood up and went for prayer, but could not just belief I was still thinking of her while praying. I managed to complete the prayer and took the food prepared for me by my sister, then went to bed when I have watched and listened to BBC network news. I woke up at midnight just because I was still thinking of her in my sleep, then I decided to put call to her and let her know how I was feeling. I picked up my phone and dialed her number, and could not't just belief she picked it up immediately as if she was expecting the call before.

Me: hello baby. How far?

Amanda: I'm fine, and you?

Me: I'm doing well too. You were not sleeping, why?

Amanda: I'm experiencing slight stomach pain. How did you know?

Me: I could notice that in your voice and again, you picked the call without any hesitation.

Amanda: don't mind me. A pot calling kettle black... What about you?

Me: I woke up to urinate and decided to remind you that you have not sent the number to me.

Amanda: number? Which number is that? Me: oh! Sorry. I wanted to say address (laughing)

Amanda: (giggled) Funny you, am very sorry for that anyway. I would do justice to that as soon as I am ok.

Me: alright then, am sorry for disturbing you by this time of the day.

Amanda: you are not disturbing me. I'm even enjoying you for keeping my company.

Me: that's lovely, but I still need to free you so as to rest a little bit because of work.

Amanda: you are such a darling! Thanks so much for being there for me.

Me: don't mind me. Take care of you.

Amanda: and you too. Bye…

Me: yeah. Bye (I hung up the call) My mind was a bit satisfied and I slept off.

I received a text message from her in the morning which stated thus; one becomes a fool and acts silly when she meets someone whom she believes, take care of you like you always say. Winks – Amanda cares about you so much. The message ignited the feelings in my heart and the feelings busted out like raging fire which water cannot quench, even flood could not stop it. I don't need any soothsayer to tell me that I'm in love. Suddenly, a thought came over me – Hope I'm not making same mistake; once beaten, twice shy is what they say… Kyle, did you even learn from your past bitter experience that made you lost your grandma? Yet, life is all about risk, at least it's a must for you to marry, only that you have to be very watchful (self motivation and encouragement.

On Saturday, Louisa called me and pleaded to me that she would not be able to make it on that day, that I should be expecting her at the end of the month.

I was neither happy nor sad on her decision since I've erased her feelings from my heart.

Louisa was the only daughter of one popular businessman in my town. She was an attractive lady with moderate bosoms and her hips were well curved.

Though, we are both from the same town but never met except one fateful day when we met in a supermarket. Her beauty caught my fancy right from that very first day. We both stared at each other at a distance, then she left and I followed her, but before catching up with her, she had entered a car, and that was when I discovered that she was brought by the car.

"We'll meet again", I said to myself and I left for house in preparation for the class as a newly admitted student.

Though, the school had resumed a month ago, but due to financial constraints, I could not resume with them at the appropriate time.

I was an orphan who did not grow up to know my parents. I was brought up by my grandmother who did petty trade to cater for us, my sister and me. And as a result of this, I hustle to meet my needs for survival.

My first day in class, I put on my best wear and looked cute, and then left for class. All eyes were on me when I entered but did not know why. I went to sit at the back since the front seats were filled up.

After some minutes, a skinny man entered and the class that was rowdy before became a graveyard. It was a lecturer, he wrote the course code on the board, MTH 121.

"Everybody should submit the last assignment I gave out", he said.

I had nothing to submit, so I was just looking.

He went through the submitted copies and said, " I know you would copy one another and I don't mind, but I will need someone among you to show what you have copied down on the board, otherwise, I will score you people zero" he threatened.

We started looking at one another, who will bail us out? I thought in my mind that I have nothing to lose since I did not submit.

He wrote the question on the whiteboard (question on permutations and combinations) which I've been thought in further mathematics when I was in high school.

I was looking at the question and at the same time thinking of the approach to use when I heard him say, "Who is belling the cat?" he asked angrily and no one stood up.

"Before the count of THREE, if someone fails to come out, you will all smell pepper", he emphasized.

Then, a guy stood up and walked up to him (we started clapping for him until when we heard what he said)

"Sir, I want to go and urinate", he said.

"You are permitted, but you are not entering my class again till the end of this session" the lecturer replied and the guy reversed to his seat.

Then, the man started counting, one, two and he was about to pronounce three when I interrupted

"Sir, though, I did not submit because I am just resuming class today, but let me give it a trial", I said soberly.

He looked down on me and said "those that were in class when the topic was been taken could not solve it, I wonder how an non serious element like you will go about it. I will allow you, but if you miss it, you have put salt to your wound", he said sarcastically.

I felt embarrassed, but I raised above the taunt and remained unruffled...

The eyes of every member of the class set on me and my heart started pounding heavily. I summoned courage, stepped forward and collected a marker from him. I drew three vertical lines to divide the board and I started proving it.

The solution was so long and tough, but thanks to God I got it. When I completed it, I wrote "QED" which means Quite Easily Done.

"This is serious! The man did it! What a perfect job! You must be a genius!" the man was flabbergasted and started to applaud while the members of the class joined him and I did not know when tears started rolling down my cheeks just because I was over joyous. The man embraced me and then asked for my name which I answered immediately. Then, he handled the submitted assignments to me said "you are the course rep of MTH 121 and you will need to follow me to my office right now", he ended the class with us and I followed him as instructed.

When we got to his office, he asked why I have not been coming to class, and I explained the challenges I was facing then. He advised and encouraged me.

I moved directly to where the departmental notice board was situated when I left his office. I stood there reading information when someone covered my eyes from the back as if we were doing hide-and-seek. I held the hands and turned around, and I could not just belief who I was looking at, it was as if I was dreaming. Could this be true?

"Were you not the one I saw in a supermarket the other day?" I asked anxiously.

"...un, yeah! You are very correct! I respect your talent" she said and put on a sumptuous smile.

"Your name, if I may ask?" I asked stylishly.

"I'm Louisa", she replied without hesitation and quickly said "Kyle, right?"

I was shocked, "how did you get to know my name?" I asked

"I was in the class when you performed a miracle in front of that wicked man called Harrison. I was very happy when you completed the work correctly, because he would not have taken it easy with you if you missed it" she said happily.

"God! So, we are course mate!" I said surprisingly.

"Yes."

"Nice meeting you", I said and handshake her

"It's my pleasure" she replied and embraced me warmly as if she had missed me a lot.

"But, why have you not been coming to class before?" she asked inquisitively

"It's a long story baby" I replied.

"But, hope you have done your registrations?" she asked.

"Not at all. I did not even know where to start", I replied.

"Hope you would not mind me putting you through?" she said while rolling her eyes and twisting her neck.

"I would appreciate it" I replied and that was how we started our friendship.

Due to the natural gift bestowed in me, people like associating themselves with me, most especially ladies but Louisa always chased them away from me and sequel to that, people saw us as lovers of which we were not, but ordinary friends.

I was emotionally connected with her after some months and I also saw the traces boldly written on her face as well, so I decided to ask her out, but she turned me down…

About 3:45pm the following day, I was still in bed and decided to switch on my phone because it was switched off in order to have sound sleep.

Immediately I switched it on, I heard it ringing, I looked at the screen and it was Louisa. I decided not to pick up her call because I was not in a good mood. She called for like five times but I refused to pick her calls. Then, she decided to send me a text message and pleaded to me to pick her calls that she just had to speak to me.

That was when I gave her second thought when she called again and I picked it up

"Hello Kyle, why are you doing this to me? It's unfair now. I've been calling your number since when we have departed but it was switched off and same thing happened this morning when I called. Was it because of my reaction yesterday night? I'm so sorry for that. To be sincere, I did not mean to hurt you", I kept mute while she continued talking, "why were you not in class today? Was it because of the issue? She asked disappointedly.

"I did not get myself right since when you told me that you are not ready for any relationship. If I was in the class, I could not concentrate, so why coming to class while I'll gain nothing?" I confessed.

"I am very sorry for hurting your feelings; I'm going to do justice about it. I'm sorry once again", she apologized and continued, "Mr. Harrison even asked of you and also said, 'we are writing his test tomorrow by 6:00pm' and I have not understood the last topic he taught us very well. So, would you be so good to come and explain it to me in my house?" she requested

"I will, but am not coming to your house. Let's meet at FF block in the school", I replied

"I know you will deny coming to my house, but no problem. When should I be expecting you?" she asked remarkably.

"Just give me some minutes" I replied soberly.

I left for bathroom and saw two missed calls when I came back. I checked it, and it was class rep, Fred. I was about to call him back when he called back...

"Hello Fred, how far?" I said."

"I am fine bro. Why were you not in class today?" he curiously asked.

"Nothing bro. I just felt like relaxing at home today" I replied.

"You are the boss of life, myself wanna be like you. Am very sure that your girl must have updated you on Mr.Popo's new development" he said remarkably.

"Who are you referring to as my girl? You guys! I have not heard from anyone, update me chap chap" I replied anxiously

"Stop pretending bro! Besides, I am calling you on behalf of the whole class to ask about your well-being and also to invite you as tutor for the tutorial which is holding in D16 by 6:00pm today", he said.

I sighed, "Tutor what? Why me: what did I know to teach you guys?" I asked interrogatively.

"I have delivered what they sent me and you must not fail us. Good day" he said and hung up the call without letting me utter a word to what he has said. I was confused. Will I be able to meet up? How do I go about Louisa's case?

"I will have to be very brief with Louisa" I said.

Then, the worms in my stomach started rumbling, but nothing to give them. I dressed up quickly and set out for school. I trekked to the street where I could get bike easily because I reside in our family house with my grandma.

I got to school after some minutes, went directly to FF block and called her.

"Hello baby, where are you?" I asked on phone

"FF5. Are you in school?" she curiously asked.

"Yeah. I'll join you shortly", with that, I heard "your call credit is exhausted" and my call was terminated. Thank God she has told me the room where she is.

I rushed upstairs by skipping some stairs and got to her within a tinkle of an eye.

They were seven in the room, three couples and she was the only one sitting alone.

She frowned at me when I entered.

"It seems you are not happy. What is the problem?" I asked in a caring manner.

"Free me! I don't know what I have done to deserve that", she said disappointedly.

I moved closer and sat beside her and then placed my left hand on her right shoulder while my right hand was used to hold her left hand leaving the right one free and tried to pet her.

"Baby, what's really the problem? I'm lost and can't even reason right. Accept my apology in case I've hurt you, just forgive me", I pleaded.

"You have changed! I just have to confess to you so as to free my mind. Why did you terminate the call some minutes ago when we have not concluded the discussion?" she asked angrily.

"I'm very sorry dear. It was not intentional, but the credit got exhausted. You should trust me that I could not't do such to you baby" I explained and tried to give the phone to her for confirmation, but she rejected it.

"Hope you are now pleased with me?" I inquired.

"I'm not yet satisfied. In fact, still not happy", she confessed bitterly.

"What is the matter again?" I asked like a wounded lion that has lost its claws and teeth.

"I've been inviting you to my house for so long but you have never honoured my invitation and same thing still repeated itself today. We have been friends for more than a month now and you have never in your life being to my house, let alone of you taking me to your house and you claimed you love me, is that love? Loving someone without bothering to know where she lives", she lamented bitterly and went crimson

I was touched by her words and also felt embarrassed when those people in the class with us set eyes on us as if they were watching drama.

I was short of words for some minutes before I could say something.

"Louisa, I'm so sorry for what I have done and I'm ready to correct my mistakes. Would you be so glad to lead me there now?" I requested like a debater who has just accepted a defeat.

I did not know where and how that sumptuous smile came from, it just appeared all over her face, it was just like a magic.

She giggled and hugged me so tightly and we zoomed off to her house which was very close to school.

On our way to her house,...

I decided to tell her that I would not stay long due to the tutorial I was invited for.

"I will just know the place today and pay you a full visit tomorrow", I said.

"So, you will not teach me what I purposely called you for before leaving?" she asked disappointedly.

"Louisa! Try and understand me now. I thought I told you that I am having tutorial with the members of our class by 6:00pm today and the tutorial will be based on what we have been taught in class, maybe you join them", I said with tremble in my voice. She looked at me disappointedly.

"And you said I am special to you! Treating your special one equally with other members of the class, no problem!" she confessed.

"I'm very sorry for my utterances baby. Just try and understand me. I did not mean to hurt you. Just pardon me" I apologized.

"I don't even know the reason why I'm doing all these. It seems am forcing you to do what you did not want to do" she said gleefully.

"Baby, I'm gonna do anything because of you just to see you happy and mind you, as from now on, I'm gonna treat you like a queen", I said and then threw my right hand on her neck and pecked her on the cheek.

She looked at me amazingly and smiled but did not utter a word till when we got to where she resided.

She opened the door and asked me to enter then she followed.

It was a bedroom flat. Her room was well set and quite cozy.

"Welcome to my hut. What should I offer you? Don't tell me you are ok", she said joyfully.

"Did I hear you say hut? In fact, this is what they should be referring to as 'heaven on earth'. If I say I'm ok, you might be thinking that I'm still annoyed with you. In the light of that, just bring anything edible" I requested to satisfy the angry worms that have been murmuring in my stomach.

She brought out a mortuary standard five alive juice from a portable freezer and two glasses.

"I'm very sorry for offering you this dear. I never believed you could be here today, had it been I know, I would have prepared you a nice food. All the same just give me some minutes to dish you something delicious" she said gleefully.

"I'm very much ok with this baby, so don't bother about that. I'm taking this one self just to show you love", I replied but I did not mean what I said because I was seriously hungry.

She stared at me for some minutes and smiled. She poured the juice into a glass cup and brought it to me because I was sitting on a chaise lounge. She went down on her knees to show some respect and offered it to me.

I was shocked and impressed, I could not just belief her type still exists.

I collected it from her and supported her up.

Louisa was a good wife material. Despite the fact that she was born with silver spoon in her mouth, yet she was humble and respectful.

I asked her to get her own glass of juice and she obeyed and we clinked the glasses happily and drank.

"Louisa, let's get the work done so that you will have enough time to revise it", I said.

"Thanks dear", she responded.

I was waiting for her to bring out her book when my phone started ringing. I looked at the screen and it was the class rep, Fred, then I picked it up...

"Bro, how far now? Are you not showing up?" he asked.

"I can't disappoint the class now. 6:00pm right?" I asked

"Yes now! This is 5:55pm by my time here, so you ought to have been here by now", he said

I was shocked when I checked my wrist watch to confirm the time.

"I will join you in the next five minutes bro", I said optimistically.

"Alright, we will be expecting you boss", he said jokingly.

"Trust me bro", I responded, he hung up the call.

We both looked at each other at the same time while there was silence.

"What is going to happen now?" she asked in pity.

I was short of words. Different things were running through my mind. What a dilemma!

"Louisa, can you just do me a favour by attending the class together with them? It will not speak well to fail the whole class. Had it been I have been taking them before, it would have been easy to reject today's offer. I promise to retake you if you don't get it in the class", I pleaded to convince her.

"I have heard you. let's go because it's already past six", she replied satisfactorily.

I was so happy and gave her a nice peck on her cheek.

"Thank you dear", I appreciated her and we zoomed off to school.

We met full house at the venue of the tutorial, everyone was set waiting for me.

"Pardon me for coming late. I'm really sorry", I apologized to the whole class for coming late.

"Apology granted. We have known and even said it before your arrival that Louisa must be the one delaying you. So just carry on with the tutorial", said Aisha, a class member.

I looked at Louisa's face and saw her smiling, and then I thanked the whole class and started the tutorial.

We finished the tutorial around 7:52pm and they appreciated me for opening their eyes to many hidden facts about the course.

I was dragged out of the place by Louisa and asked me to follow her back to her house. I accompanied her and petted her to let me go home because grandma must have been expecting me since I did not tell her I was not coming home on that day.

"Call her you are not coming home today now", she said.

"She is not connected", I replied.

"You mean, she does not have phone?" she questioned doubtfully.

"No, she does not", I replied.

She kept mute for some seconds.

"Don't let me delay you then, we shall talk tomorrow. Remember to greet her for me and take care of yourself too", she said and handed a note book to me to keep for her till the following day. I was in hurry so I could not question her on the book.

"Thanks for the understanding. Take care of you too" I replied and stopped a bike which took me to my abode.

I was seriously tired and wanted to rest, but it was hot so I decided to put off my wear. In that process my phone started ringing, I checked who was calling and it was her. I managed to pick up the call...

"Hello dear, hope you are now at home?" she asked in a caring tone.

"Yeah, just now. Thanks for the care", I replied.

"You are the one to thank most. How is grandma doing?" she asked.

"Fine, she is on bed already", I replied.

"Ah! So, what are you gonna eat tonight or she has prepared you something to eat?" she questioned in a caring tone.

"I have not checked. I'm gonna take care of myself. Thanks for the care. What about you?" I asked in return.

"I'm ok. Have you opened the book?" she asked anxiously.

"No, what is it for?" I curiously asked.

"Whatever you see when you open it is yours. Good night", she said and hung up the call.

I quickly picked up the book and checked. I could not just believe what I
saw.

This is serious! Five thousand dollars notes! Is she trying to bribe me or she did it out of love? "Definitely, Louisa wanted to hang up on me but just trying to pretend. Even the way she reacted to me today shows she is in love with me", I have the thought in my mind.

I was so happy and decided to put a call to her, but her number was not reachable and I later dropped her text message of appreciation.

I had a splendid night rest that day.

I called her very early in the morning to ask about her night and also thanked her and she was very happy to hear from me at that very moment.

I prepared for school and ate the food prepared for me by grandma and left for school.

We had non-stopped lectures from 8:00am till 4:00pm that day and the remaining two hours was used to revise with Louisa in her room before we went back to school for the test.

While in the test hall, I had finished my work within a short period of time and cross checking was on when I heard a lady's voice calling my name and I was about to turn my neck to the direction where the voice came from when Mr. Harrison caught me and asked me to submit. And since I have finished it, I did not bother to say anything; I just submitted it and left the hall.

After some minutes, he instructed everybody to submit and they started coming out one after the other. Most of them came to thank me because the questions were almost the same as the ones we solved at the tutorial. The man only changed some values.

When Louisa came out, she was over joyous and hugged me so tight in the presence of other members of the class. I felt embarrassed but nothing could be done than to take it that way. She held my right hand and dragged me towards her house.

We kept on chatting as we were going and we were about to exit the school gate when I heard a deep voice call my name. We both looked at the back at a time and it was a huge guy putting on a blue jean and a black round neck top, Gift, a member of the class.

Louisa and I halted while he worked to us.

"Louisa, excuse us. I want talk to Kyle", he commanded and she abided immediately by taking some steps forward.

"What make you submit quickly like that? Because you know am well, then you are now showing off? Or you do not know that is because of what you did that make the man to collect the scripts from us quickly? I just want to advise you not to do such again. If you finish, keep it and let us finish too", he advised in threatening tone.

"Bro, don't be angry. Myself don't want to submit, but when I want to discuss with someone who ask from me, that's when he saw me and ask me to submit. It will not happen again bro" I explained and pleaded.

"No problem, I just want you to adjust", he said emphatically.

"Trust me bro", I replied optimistically.

He handshake me and headed back to where he was coming from.

I went back to Louisa and we zoomed off to her house.

"What was he discussing with you?" she asked inquisitively.

"I will gist you when we get home", I replied.

"Hope no problem?" she inquired.

"Not really dear", I replied.

When we got to her house, I was seriously tired and at the same time feeling hungry, so I just stretched myself on the chaise lounge.

" tell me what you promised me o", she curiously asked and I tried to explained to her.

"What did he mean? How does your own life affect his? I can't take this. Never! Authority must hear this! And if anything should happen to you, I will hold him responsible and his family gotta pay for it as well", she lamented angrily.

"Take it easy dear. Nothing will happen by God's grace. It's only that I have to know how to be playing my games in the class", I calmed her down.

"Alright then, I heard you. Just lend me two minutes to get pepper at the gate. I supposed to buy it when we were coming, but I was carried away by your words", she said and rolled her eyes.

"Ok, May I accompany you?" I asked with weak voice.

"Don't bother, I can see you are very tired. I will be back shortly", she said in a caring tone, pecked me and left...

It was getting dark. I waited for her arrival for some minutes but I could not hear her foot step. I picked up my phone so as to call her and I heard her phone ringing on the bed.

Oh my God! She did not go with her phone.

I decided to trace her to gate where she claimed she wanted to buy pepper.

When I got to the school gate, I could not just believe what I saw. The obituary of Mr. Harrison was pasted at the entrance of the school gate. How come? Mr. Harrison! He conducted a test for us today! Never! I wiped my face with my palm to confirm if I was dreaming, but it was not. I felt like crying, then, I managed to control myself and asked one of the on-looker beside me what caused his death.

"I learnt that he was murdered by a sect of cultist when he was heading to his house", she said gently and left the spot immediately.

"Oh my God! Why this?" I said with full sense of concern.

Then, I was trying to search for Louisa amongst the crowd when my phone started ringing, I looked at the screen and it was an unknown number, then I picked it up the call...

"Hello, is this Kyle on the line please?"

"Yes, I'm Kyle. Who's this please?" I replied in an effort to recognize the voice, when he spoke out again.

"It's me Aisha, your course mate", she muttered.

"Oh ooh, Aisha, how are you doing?" I asked, even when I was surprised at why she would be calling me at the late hours of the day.

"Where are you?" she curiously asked.

"I'm at the small gate of the school", I replied.

"Ok, about that of Mr. Harrison?" she asked in a sympathetic way.

"Yes, in fact it shocked me", I replied in pain.

"You know what? You will have to meet us at the school medical immediately!" she exclaimed rushing to hang up, but I quickly asked her to hold on.

"Wait, wait, what's the problem, what happened?" interrupting her just before she hung up.

"Louisa was found almost lifeless at the school gate and she has been rushed to the school medical centre. Please meet us up at the medical centre immediately." she said and hung up.

Her last words hit me hard; I was shocked and almost fainted at what she just disclosed.

Could it be that Gift had started out his plans against me through Louisa or because of Mr. Harrison's death? I reasoned with shock, my brain had gone blank as I pondered over it.

I left the spot where I was and picked a race to the medical.

On getting there, I met almost every member of my class outside. Most of the ladies there started crying when I arrived while the guys quickly held me.

"Please, what has happened to Louisa? Where is she?" I questioned with tremble in my voice while my hands and legs were shaking like a vibrator.

In that process, a doctor came out and told us that she has started responding to treatment, but we need to leave the premises or we keep mute.

"I need just only two guys to follow me", he said.

Then, everybody got relaxed. Fred and I decided to follow him and he took us to where she was receiving treatment.

Her head was bandaged. It was not more than two minutes that we got there, she started breathing heavily and we quickly called on doctor, but before the doctor could come around...

She had stopped the breathing and the doctor said she has given up the ghost. On hearing that, I fainted immediately and the next thing I discovered was that, I was tapped by Louisa, and then I woke up from my slumber. I was shocked and shouted "Yeh! Yeh!! Ghost, ghost!", then I was about to rush out when she grabbed me and started asking…

"What is the matter? What happened? What's the problem now", she kept on wondering while I was still panting heavily like someone who was pursued by a masquerade.

She held me tightly, placed her head on my chest and tears started rolling down from her eyes and that was when I knew I was still in her room. So, it was a dream! I hugged her tightly and I started weeping as well. My weep was not because of anything, but the love I have for her was inestimable which got me scared by the horror dream because I was afraid of losing her.

"It was a dream. I'm now ok dear. Am very sorry for scaring you", I said to her in a fairing tone.

She looked into my eyes while I did same thing. I could see love burning in her eyes like a raging fire.

We stared at each other for some seconds and before we knew anything, we had started kissing. I kissed her lips tenderly while we closed our eyes as I felt the warm taste of her lips……

But she soon got herself and gently pushed away my face, while she looked at me gratefully, and with shinning eyes.

"I have never felt this way before thank you" she said, while she looked away and closed her eyes briefly. I equally felt something strong when we kissed, which I have never felt in my life because I had never been into any relationship before.

She stood up and asked me to join her in eating what she had prepared which I did because I was seriously hungry.

Despite the fact that I was seriously hungry, I was still unable to concentrate on the food I was eating after she broke the kiss, because all my thoughts were now on her, and I knew she was feeling same way. I still wanted her kiss so badly, but yet I had to control myself, because she is nothing but a humble girl who has her pride and dignity to protect, and so I washed my hands and stood up minutes later, while she stared at me which made me almost lost focus...

"Where are you going to?" she asked with a smile, while he equally stood up as well

and held my hand.

"Am now ok. Thanks so much for today. I have to leave now. Am very sure grandma must have been waiting for me", I replied.

She stared at me for some minutes.

"You and grandma all the time. Grandma's pet. I will like to know her one of these days", she said jokingly while still holding my hands.

"it would be nice", I responded in an appreciating tone.

She placed her hands on my shoulders and stared at my face again...

"Are you coming to my house tomorrow as well", she asked with a pleading face, while I looked up.

"I will try" I replied, but instead of letting me go, she drew closer to me, pulled my face with her palms and kissed me again, while my soul melted and I did not know when I kissed her back briefly before pushing me away.

I immediately fled her room without looking back and she ran after me thinking I had took it up with her, but I let her knew it was because I was late and she became calm.

I was very fortunate that night because I could get a bike immediately I got out of her house…

I got home around quarter to ten and met grandma outside waiting for my arrival...

"What kept you so late?" she curiously asked.

"we did a test and we were doing the correction and also, I visited a friend of mine when we finished", I replied.

"but, you are too long" she confessed.

"am sorry" I apologized and we went in.

She had prepared me what to eat as usual, but I could not take it because of what I had eaten with Louisa.

I was about to enter my room when my phone started ringing and it was no other person than Louisa. I smiled and picked up her call...

"Hello dear, are you now at home?" she asked with care.

"Yea.Just now. I even met grandma outside waiting for me", I replied.

"Eh! Hope she did not get mad at you?" she inquired.

"Not at all", I replied.

"Thank God. Kyle, I really appreciate you for today, in fact, you really made my day. Thanks so much", she appreciated joyfully.

"Are you the one to thank me? I'm in the right position to do that", I replied jokingly.

"I know you don't like hearing such" she said.

"Don't mind me", I replied.

"Dear, you know what?" she asked in a tender voice.

"I don't, except you tell me", I replied jokingly.

"We have to see tomorrow because I have an important issue to discuss with you regarding to our studies and the relationship", she said in a serious mood.

"We gonna discuss it tomorrow after class. Hope it's not that serious?" I said in fair manner.

"To me, it's not, but I don't know what is gonna be your opinion", she replied.

"Can't we just discuss it on phone now?" I anxiously asked.

"It's not what we can discuss on phone. Be calm. To be sincere, it's not a serious matter", she said calmly.

I sighed, "No problem then. Catch you tomorrow", I replied unsatisfactorily.

"Good night. Don't forget to dream about me. Love you", she said excitedly.

"And you too. Love you to the bones", I reciprocated it and she hung up the call.

It was a cool Friday morning. We had only one lecture to receive on that day and it was to hold from 9:00am to 12:00 noon. It was a 4units course and the lecturer In charge did not joke with his attendance.

I left for class and sat at the back gazing at Louisa at the front. We were all waiting for the lecturer in charge to come when the course representative's phone started ringing. He asked us to keep mute that it was the lecturer and we abided.

After some minutes, she hung up the call, and faced the class and smirked…

"Ladies and gentlemen, am using this medium to inform you that today's lecture is not going to hold…

We all shouted interrupted "oh…." and some people have started leaving the class immediately without bothering to hear her last word.

"Listen now", she shouted at us and continued, "You did not even allow me to land before leaving. Did you know if what I wanted to say was 'is not going to hold here, but another venue", she said aggressively and on hearing that, almost everyone kept quiet except for those that were murmuring.

In fact, I like the lady due to her courageous attitude.

She cleared her baritone and said "the man said, 'we should meet on Monday'" and left the class immediately.

The class became rowdy and some people started throwing abusive words to the lady.

I stood up from where I sat and started moving towards Louisa when she was trying to make a call and then, my phone started ringing. She turned to the back and grinned when she saw me…

☆☆

She wrapped her arm round my waist and dragged me out of the class. I was somehow timid because I was not use to such way of life. We left the school for her house. I sat on my permanent place in her room which was chaise longue.

She started moving up and down in order to offer me what to eat, but I told her not to bother herself.

"let's discuss what you called me for yesterday night" I said gently.

"A minute please", she said hurriedly and tuned on her television, inserted one Korean film into DVD set and then sat on the bed directly opposite to me, and she started…

"To be sincere, I don't even know where and how to start this issue, but let me put it this way" she said while I was staring at her, she continued, "but Kyle, can't you just be living with me here instead of going to and fro everyday? I don't like the way you stress yourself going up and down and how you leave me most of the time when you are needed the most" while saying that she maintained her eye contact and her gesticulation was good enough to explain herself.

I took a deep breath, "if I say I did not understand what you were trying to say, that means I'm a liar. I also wished to reside very close to school, but due to what I have once told you which was financial constraints", I paused and sighed. Then, I gazed and I saw something very unusual and I froze! Right before me; at the very particular spot where she sat on the bed; her legs were parted and weirdly spread; slightly angled towards me with her skirt ridden up to her mid-thigh!

Was she presenting me an open up skirt? I had to quickly pull away my eyes, reassess the situation to reassure myself that this was reality and not a dream.

I returned my gaze but not to that previous spot but to her face and there she was looking at me in the face, telling her story of which I was not following anymore and maintaining a radiant smile. I have to be sure it was a mistake on her own part and have to stare again at the parted legs, certainly she would trace and follow my stare as I did. And yes they were still parted and in fact more revealing. I could now see her inner thighs and the various ridges that formed its roundness. I was lost in confusion.

In fact, at some point, her legs were much separated that I could easily see the terrain of her puffy pussy on her white doted panties!! I was taken and I so much knew that she was aware I was watching and possibly encouraged it!! This was totally killing and made me lost totally.

I could feel my joystick nodding hard and the boxer was already wet.

I did not know what to do due to the fact that it was my first time in such scenario.

She gazed at me and stood up...

... And came to sit beside me. Louisa really was the kind of lady most guys do dream of, because not only was she good Looking and wealthy, she also was the free type. I knew she really loved me, but the problem was just her manner of approach. She was scared of making the first move, which was then left in my hands to encourage her decently, because I wanted her but did not know how to go about it. Suddenly, I did not know what came over me. I carried her up, kissed her for a while, before gently laying her on her bed, and we stared at each other, while my eyes melted as her heavy gaze went all through my body which sent cold down my spine...

She pulled off her top, while I stared at her blossom with surprise, and my face coloured up as I swallowed hard. "I'm all yours, but please be gentle with me" she said to me, while she gave me a weird look. "Hope you are sure about this?" I asked, she drew down my face and kissed me. "Yea as long as you promise to keep your word that you will never abandon me" she replied, while she smiled deeply. "I swear with my life baby, I will never leave you as long as I'm alive" I swore. "Then I'm all yours sweetheart" she said with a wink, while I smiled, and gently pulled off her bra.....

Her hot lips were soon on me and well, that she was immediately carried away by sweet pleasure she closed her eyes, as I worked on her, and it just felt as if we were the only people in the world. My trouser was soon on the floor, my boxer followed minutes later and before I could even breath twice, I was already on her. I got to know she was also a virgin when I was trying to insert my joystick into her honey pot but could not get through on time. It took me some minutes before the way was through and before she could beg me to take it easy, she felt a sharp pain in her body which made her screamed and almost withdrew herself. She gasped, opened her eyes and tried to push me away but I was stronger than her....

I thrust in again and again, while she dug her fingers on my chest as she endured the pain silently because the expression was written on her face. I kept on enjoying it as I was thrusting gently while she was caressing me and groaning gently. I really tried that day as I did my best. She tenderly kissed me, and I did not know how I felt that moment because it was as if I was on top of the world. "Please stop it's okay" she finally pleaded as she strongly held me, while I gazed into her eyes and jerked as if something had pushed me from behind, before lying on top of her. She closed her eyes as we both breathed deeply and gently. She pushed me away. "I'm so sorry for hurting you" I apologized as I felt her face with his palms, while she unsuccessfully tried to fight back tears which finally dripped out of her eyes. Why was she crying? I knew not, but I thought because she gave me her body willingly and not under duress, but I guess the feeling of losing her most cherished treasure made her cried. Truthfully she really was very romantic, which equally increased the love I had for her. Oh she simply was an angel that day...

It took us like thirty minutes before we could talk to each other because we both felt ashamed of what we have done.

"Dear, I'm sorry for what has happened. I promise to keep my words", I said to break the silence and pulled her up.

She looked at me in wonders and tears started rolling down again. Then, I quickly fought back the tears and embraced her, planted a kiss on her forehead and then sat her down on the chaise longue.

I removed the bed-spread and soaked it in a pail half filled with water because it was a bit stained and then lead her to the bathroom where we both took our bath.

Thereafter, we regained our usual way of life. She prepared spice and chicken which we ate together like a couple and decided to watch movies together after the meal, and that was when she brought up the issue of living together again…

"Dear, you are sleeping here tonight", she said without looking at my face.

"If that should be the case, then I will need to go home and inform grandma", I replied.

On hearing that, she was very happy and pecked my chin…

"Thanks dear. Love you so much", she said joyfully.

"Love you more than you do", I replied.

"Really?" she rolled her eyes and asked.

"Trust me", I affirmed.

"We are going there together, so as to use that opportunity to know who have been taking care of you for me", she said.

"No problem dear", I replied.

She stood up and leaned forward to her wardrobe, and came back to me with certain amount of money which she stylishly put in the back pocket of my trouser. I dodged it out and asked what to use the money for, and she said I should use it to get a phone for grandma. I tried to reject it but she refused to have it back saying it was not meant for me but for grandma and I succumbed to her excuse.

When it was 5:15pm, we set out for our plan. We bought a phone and a SIM card which was registered immediately.

When we got home, I introduced her to my grandma while she went on her knees and grandma prayed for her.

I did not tell her that we will be staying together, instead I told her I've gotten a room on rent very close to my school and she supported.

I knew that grandma would not miss me too much because I happened to be a hustler and did not normally stay at home with her.

We packed some of my belongings like wears and shoes into a leather bag and moved out. She offered grandma a certain amount of money before we left.

She carried the bag for me and we were moving to the nearby junction where we could get a bike when we heard "Louisa", a lady's voice from behind. We were both shocked and looked at the back at a time... Louisa's reaction turned moody when she saw her...

"A minute please", Louisa said and went to her while I stood still wondering…

"what could be the relationship between both of them; why did Louisa's reaction turned moody? But she is the first and the last in her family which means Sophia can't be her sister, so why was she afraid?" I was engrossed in my thoughts when I heard an elongated hiss from Sophia which caught my attention. She looked down on me from afar and walked out on Louisa.

I suspected she has poisoned her (Louisa) mind because I was expecting her to join me but she was only standing still looking sober, depressed and helpless. I walked up to her and asked her what the problem was…

"Dear, what's the problem?" I asked with a great concern written all over my face.

"Baby, to be sincere I could not get myself right for now. I'm very sorry I will not be able to tell you anything for now. Let's go home please", she replied while standing akimbo.

I was short of words, so I did not bother to disturb her further until when we got home.

"Louisa, look at my face", I said and she did, "who is Sophia to you?" I asked inquisitively while staring at her.

She was shocked, "she is my cousin and we stayed together before I was offered admission into this school. Did you know her before or how did you get to know her name?" she explained and asked anxiously. Then, she started gaining her lost courage and freedom.

"Yeah, very well. She was my high school mate and a companion then, but suddenly turned to a foe just because she loved me and wanted us to take our friendship beyond, but which I rejected it", I replied.

"But why did not you go into relationship with her if I may ask?" she stylishly asked.

"it was due to the fact that I did not love her, and also, I was in love with my studies and did not want to get involved in any love affair which could distract my attentions. In additional to that, she was rude and people complained about her alot", I explained.

"That's serious! No wonder! Hun! Now, I got it!", she exclaimed and shook her head in affirmation to what I said.

"No wonder what?" I asked anxiously.

"Don't worry about that dear. All I know is that, what God has joined together, no one dare put asunder. Therefore, let's move on with our life and forget about her issue", she said daringly.

I could deduce what Sophia has told her from her words, but since she has assured me of her feelings, then, I succumbed to what she said and we started living as a couple.

Our love became the talk of the campus. We even won the best couple of the year in our department.

All of a sudden, my academic performance started dropping and my CGPA dropped drastically and as a result of that, I lost the opportunity of becoming a scholar which could have earned me alot of benefits.

******

Some days after convocation, we both went to our various homes.

I woke up following the call of my Love one fateful Saturday. She told me she threw up a day before that day and when she went for test, it was discovered that she was pregnant.

It was a big slap on my face when I had what she said...

"Are you joking or what?" I inquired inquisitively.

"Common! How do you expect me to joke with costly issue such as this?" she questioned.

I took a deep breath...

"where did you carry out the test?" I gently asked.

"I conducted it myself when I could not see my period and it was positive", she replied.

I was lost and confused...

"So, what are we gonna do now?" I asked.

"That's why am calling you to seek your opinion", she replied.

"Have you informed your Dad?" I asked.

"My dad? You want to kill me. He must not here about this except you want me dead", she replied irritatingly.

"where did you carry out the test?" I asked out of tension forgotten that I have asked her before.

She was so furious about my reaction towards the issue

"Are your ears not functioning again or how many times will I tell you I did it myself?" she replied angrily.

"Be calm now! At least you brought this issue to me because I am involved and you have believe in my words, so why lashing me with such words?" I fired back.

She became calm and almost cried on phone.

"I'm sorry for that. I did not mean to throw such words unto you, but I was frustrated. So, your opinion?" she apologized and requested for the way out.

"To be sincere, I did not know what to say since you said your Dad must not hear about it", I said, while expecting her to decide.

"I can't leave it. I will find solution to it myself. It's just that I have to get you informed before going into it", she said boldly.

I was shocked and can't just belief what I heard from her. So, I need to confirm it.

"Are you trying to say you gonna abort it?" I asked with tremble in my voice.

"I don't have any other alternative than that", she affirmed her stand.

"Did you even think of the danger of what you want to embark on? We have to see each other and discuss because I am not in support of that your decision", I confessed.

"I'm ready for the worst, so no need to discuss anything my dear. Be good and stay out of worry. I'm gonna be fine", she said and tried to console me.

I know there is nothing I could say to convince her. That's the only BUT she has, once she decides on a particular thing, only death can stop her from doing it.

"But, I am still interested in seeing you", I said in sober mood.

"My dad is around for now, so I'll give you a call to tell you the new development later", she replied and hung up the call.

I wiped my face to confirm if it was a dream, but it was a reality. I stood up from the bed and started wandering in the room thinking on what could be the outcome of her decision.

I was physically and emotionally disturbed when I waited for her call but did not see her brake light, and then decided to call her while she refused to pick it up.

When it was around 8:55pm that very day, my phone started ringing and quickly looked at the screen to check if it was her, but it was an unknown number...

I picked it up without hesitation…

"hello, is this Kyle please?"

"yes, I am Kyle. Who's this please?" I replied in an effort to recognize the voice, when he spoke out again.

"It's me James, your paddy", he muttered.

"oh oh, James how far now?" I asked, even when I was surprised that why is he calling me at the late hours of the day and not using his number.

"Where are you?" he curiously asked.

"I'm at home right now. Any gist?" I inquired.

"You know what? You will have to vacate your house immediately in order to avoid being arrested!" he exclaimed rushing to hang up, but I quickly ask him to hold on…

"wait wait, what's the problem, what happened?" interrupting him just before he hung up.

"Based on what I heard, Louisa was found almost lifeless in her room bleeding heavily. It was discovered that she aborted and she has been brought to my father's clinic. And it seemed her father has ordered for your arrest", he explained and hung up.

His last word hit me hard which got me shocked and almost collapsed at what he just disclosed.

My mood was destabilized and I did not know the next line of action to seek redress.

I stood at akimbo and I did not know when I started crying. Suddenly, I heard a knock on the door which got me shocked and sent a cold down my spine. I started panting and quickly hide at the back of the door. I heard the knock again and a voice followed...

"Kyle, what happened? Open the door".

Then, I became calm and quickly wiped the tears and pretended as if nothing has happened. I opened the door for her and she sat on my bed asking me what the problem was. She was too precious to me and it was hard for me to hide anything from her, so I explained everything to her.

She was highly disappointed in me and wept for my mistake. She asked me to pack immediately that very night and find somewhere to hide so as not to get arrested.

When I was ready to flee, her eyes was saturated with tears and she hugged me so tight and then dissolved into tears. I was touched and I started weeping too. I felt like staying with her, but she released me and prayed for me.

I later summoned courage like a gallant soldier and left the house without heading to any particular destination.

I called James's number but it was not available and I decided to go directly to his house since it was dark and fortunately for me, I met him at home.

He asked me on how it happened which I explained to him and he counseled me to leave the town as early as possible because Louisa's dad was very wicked and he could do anything to get me eliminated due to what has happened to his one and only child.

On hearing that, my heart started pounding heavily and had a restless night due to the challenges ahead of me.

Very early the following day at about 5:05am, I left the town.

When I got to the my sister town, I looked for my sister who was also struggling for survival and got her informed about the situation on ground. She seemed carefree and less concerned about me.

Then, that was when I decided to put a call to grandma…

She picked up the call but it was a man's voice. I dropped the call so as to confirm if I have dialed the right number, and yes I was correct. Then, I re-dialed it and it was that same voice…

"Hello, who am I on to?" I asked with a great concern.

"This is sergeant Foss from Cambridge police station, division 2, speaking on behalf of Kyle mom", he answered.

I was shocked to hear that grandma has been arrested just because of the issue.

"But what has she done to deserve that? How dare you arrest an elderly innocent woman?" I questioned aggressively.

"Hear this fool! You had better show up before it is too late for you" he said in concise way.

I was short of words and then hung up the call.

"You have landed my mom into trouble through your stupid act" my sister said while I looked at her with horror eyes.

She took her phone and called grandma's number again and pleaded to the sergeant to let her speak with her and which he allowed.

She (grandma) told my sister not to let me show up, that she is ready to bear whatever comes out of it. My sister was not satisfied with her decision and hung up the call angrily.

After three days, my sister decided to go home in order to check her (grandma) and she came back with sad news which landed me in hospital.

"When I got home, I went straight to Louisa's dad and pleaded to him to set my mom free and which he did by giving me a letter to the police station, but when I got there, I learnt that she has been mistakenly taken for a woman who killed her husband just because he did not take her out for valentine. And an attempt was made to correct the mistake, but she had been hanged to death before the correction could be made" she explained and busted into tears.

When I heard that, I slumped and fainted.

I woke up after some hours and still can't believe grandma has gone to the land of no return. I cried bitterly not because of anything, but because I was responsible for her death.

"Yah God, forgive me for not letting her reap the fruits of her labour and being responsible for her death by hanging", I prayed and asked for forgiveness.

It took me some days before I could recover.

Aftermath, I decided to put a call to Louisa, but her lines were switched off and likewise childhood friend's (James) number. The life became misery because I did not know if she survived it or not, but I later motivated myself and learned to move on.

I started another way of life and lost my phone in the process, I got another line neglecting the former one. I applied for direct entry into a federal university and which I was admitted.

After a year, my sister got married and relocated to New York city while I was still schooling in Town. I later joined her in New York city where she secured me a placement for my Industrial training (IT).

That was how I lost Louisa's contact and met Amanda, the banker...

It was a cool Sunday morning. I got a message from Amanda and when I read through, it happened to be the address she promised to send and that reminds me that I have an appointment with her by 12:00 noon that very day.

I quickly engaged myself in some domestic works at home and later dressed up in line with the preparation for her house.

I appeared in my favourite colours which were white and black, a well ironed white T-shirt and a black pair of trousers with black shining shoe. I checked my dressing in a standing mirror and it was classic.

"Yeah Kyle, you are good to go", I said to myself, and then informed my sister I am going out.

"This look is charming. I'm very sure you are visiting your girl today. Wait, wait, let me give you a nice shot", she said and quickly brought out her smart phone and snapped me. I looked at the picture and, I was attracted by the picture. I left the house and trekked a bit before I could get a bike. I described where I was going for the bike man and he claimed he knows the place and we agreed on a particular amount.

I checked at my golden wrist watch and it was almost noon, then, my phone started ringing. I looked at the screen and it was Amanda, then I picked it up...

"Hello dear, are you not coming again?" she asked.

"Am on my way", I replied.

"Really?" she asked anxiously.

"Yes. You suppose to have been hearing the sound of the bike", I replied.

"Yeah! yeah! Thanks dear. Expecting you" she said happily.

"Alright, I will soon be with you", I said.

"I can't wait", she replied.

"Ok ", I said and allowed her to drop the call.

"Here I come" I said to myself, standing opposite a yellow bungalow house doing nothing but contemplating whether to go in or not because I was expecting her to wait for me outside. I stared at the window hoping to catch a glimpse of the one I was seeking but saw nothing.

Although my instinct urged me to turn back when I thought about the memory I spent with Louisa but eventually my heart could not just allow me. The door bell rang melodiously when it felt my touch. I waited for a reply but I did not hear one until the second time when a feminine voice spoke from the inside.

A few minutes later, when the door was opened, I was stunned by the sight I behold, the figure standing before me was that light skinned damsel with an extravagance attire. Her charming smile was so sumptuous like that of Louisa which took me to her memory lane.

The surprise on her face was enormous when she saw me; we stood staring at each other for seconds before I broke the silence. 'Hello Amanda, it's nice seeing you' I greeted.

'Oh Kyle, is this the real you? You are seriously looking good. Oh my goodness!" she shot arrows of flattering words before I was ushered in.

"How are you doing?" I asked looking into her pale face.

She ignored my question and went inside. She came back moments later with two cups containing a bluish liquid and offered one to me which I rejected. She looked at me weirdly and rolled her eyes...

"Are you feeling shy or what? Don't tell me you are not taking anything", she said.

"Don't mind me . I'm just ok for now but promise you to take something before I take my leave", I replied.

I wondered if what I said was special when she stood up happy, sat at the edge of the chair where I was sitting and offered me a nice peck on my cheek.

The peck sent a cold down my spine and my heart melted. I wanted to turn to her just to look at her face when my eyes noticed that her skirt ridden up to her mid-thigh! She was presenting me an up skirt while looking at her pale thigh, "This lady is beautiful, I had to say and she has a body to kill. The camisole top she had over her upper half was crimson red and dropped rather low, giving me the deepest cleavage I had ever seen" I thought in my mind and I had to quickly pull away my eyes and control myself. I finally looked at her face while she smiled and winked at me. Though, I was in love before, but did not know what came over me that particular moment. I frowned at her and changed my seat.

She was shocked and confused. She joined me on my new seat..

"What's wrong? What have I done wrong? Or was it because of my attitude? I reacted that way just because am in love with you and seriously in need of you. I was expecting you to reciprocate the feelings. I'm not an non serious type and I am ready to settle down with you and deliver all my kids to you. I have been praying and waiting to see a man like you and I believed my prayer has been answered, so please and please, don't turn me down", she confessed out of worried, written all over her face while she was on her knees holding my hands.

In fact, the way she reacted enabled me to know how effective the power of love is. I looked into her eyes and I saw a gentle love like dove.

Love is as powerful as death; it drives people crazy while some have even lost their lives because of it.

I was convinced with her actions and words which forced me to open up to her about my past relationship with Louisa.

"Each time I remember grandma's death, I become sad and felt like not engaging in any relationship again", I added.

She tried to convince me further to forget about my past and try to move on.

In fact, she was really endowed because her words were so inspired.

She looked at me out of sympathy for some minutes and before I know it, her lips came crushing against mine. Our tongues fought the war of supremacy as we twisted, entwined and entangled it in action. I knew where it was heading to but I could not stop myself. I wanted the sex because its being long I have had it and I was no more a novice in the act. I lifted her feet as our lips was still in action, carrying her as we both found our way to unknown destination, dropping one piece of clothing here and there. We were almost unclad when we got to her bed.

My hands reached for her two bare bosoms, as I gently caressed them, sending shock waves down her spine, making her moan softly.

I was not a professional in the act, neither was I a virgin.

She carefully zipped down my trousers, making me completely naked and took my joystick into her hands, rubbing and working it up and down softly. I reacted by groaning softly giving her the impression that I was really enjoying it.

When I could not take it any longer, I started sucking her hard nipples while my index finger was working on her clitoris gently. She left my joystick and started begging me to insert my joystick into her honey pot and which I did without hesitation.

We both enjoyed the game together. In fact she was good and experienced on bed. After the battle, I went to bathroom to take my bath and before I came back, I have gotten three missed calls on my phone and when I checked, it was Louisa. My heart vibrated and my conscience started disturbing me. Though, I did not know whether she is engaged as well, but the fault should not be from me.

I was confused whether to call her back or not. Then, Amanda called me to join her in eating what she had prepared. I wanted to resist, but due to the promise which I made that I'm gonna eat something before leaving her, so I joined her with my troubled mind.

While eating together, she tried to feed me but which I rejected...

"What's the problem now? I've noticed you since you came back from the bathroom; it seems you are not happy. What has happened or I did not perform up to your expectation?" she asked with a great worry written all over her face.

I was about to answer her when my phone started ringing again, and it was Louisa's call. I was staring at my phone when Amanda spoke, "pick it now", and that was when I managed to pick it...

"Hello dear, where did you put your phone before?" she asked.

"I'm sorry. I left it in the room while I was in the bathroom", I replied.

"And you did not see my missed calls?" she asked.

"I saw it and I have the intention of calling you back before I was being called by a friend, so I'm very sorry", I replied.

While chatting with her over the phone, Amanda left her place and came to my side which I did not understand why she did. I neglected her and continued the chat...

"Who is that your friend?" she asked anxiously.

"A new friend, so you can't know her", I replied "but I thought you said you are coming here by ending?" I quickly asked so as to deviate from what she was asking me.

"Yeah. We need to see and talk. Hope we are still together?" she stylishly asked.

I did not know what to utter as a response, I looked at Amanda's face while she returned her look with horror face.

"I'm in the position to ask you that, but not withstanding, I'm still yours, but we need to see and talk as you said", I replied feeling uncomfortable.

"Really? I trust you and that's why I love you", she said happily and she hung up by saying "love you" which I replied "love you too".

I dropped my phone on the table and took a deep breath.

"Good of you! Well done! I'm very sure that person was Louisa. Now, tell me, where I belong because I could hear all your conversation?" she asked.

I was in dilemma and short of words.

"It seems I'm using myself to beg you? I want you to listen and listen well; I can't lose you to Louisa. It's either you marry both of us together or she leaves you for me. I'm ready to give it whatever it takes" she threatened.

I sat down with my head buried in my thoughts and almost cried because of the challenge before me.

She held me tight and raised my head

"I'm very sorry for my words. I did not mean to hurt you, but I can't let go of you because I'm in love already. If I had known that this is how it will be, I would not have agreed with her. Now, it has turned to something else which is difficult for me to get over", she confessed while crying.

I was lost and confused with her confession, "if she had known, she would not have agreed with her" who was she referring to? I asked myself...

EPISODE 30

I summoned courage and challenged her

"What did I hear you say just now? Who were you referring to?" I asked irritatingly.

She wiped her tears with her back hand.

"Let's forget about that. All I know is that, things are going to be well", she replied courageously.

Then, the pressure on me has gone a bit and my mind was a little bit free. I looked at the wall clock and it was quarter to six. There was rumbling of thunder outside which made me peeped through the window and it was about to rain.

"Amanda, I have to leave", I said in a hurry.

"But we still need to talk", she replied.

"Yeah, we are still together now", I said while putting on my shoe.

"No problem then", she replied unsatisfactorily while I jumped out of the house. I was fortunate to get a bike going to my area, but the amount was double, and since I was in a hurry so as not to be caught up by the rain, I agreed and he took me to my destination safely before the commencement of the heavy rain which stopped around 11:15pm.

When I got home, I got my sister informed about the scenario so as to put me through on the issue and our conversation went thus;

Sister: You said you just met Amanda a week ago

Me: yes ma.

Sister: how come she quickly gets involved to the extent of planning a family with you without even knowing where you stay? Moreover, you're still schooling.

Me: that's exactly what is giving me headache too. I did not even know from whom I inherited that, because I wonder why ladies are after me despite the fact that I have nothing to offer them.

Sister: you inherited it from our father. I have once heard it from my mom that ladies do disturb our father when he was alive.

Me: what should I do now?

Sister: you will need to see Louisa first and confirm if she is still in love with you and has not chosen.

Me: yes now! I know she is still in love. In fact, she needs me seriously.

Sister: don't say that. Someone you have left for the past three years and you are still putting all your trust in her, and besides she does not deserve you because her father should be held responsible for grandma's death.

On hearing that, I felt discouraged. "Is my sister trying to support Amanda and discourage me from Louisa", I said to myself and I need to know her stand sequel to Louisa issue.

Me: but sister, assuming I later go for Louisa, won't you support?

Sister: what will be Amanda's faith? Why did you sleep with her when you know that Louisa is still coming back? Or you counted her cheap just because she showed you love? You had better think of it very well and stop taking her feelings for granted. Don't forget, what goes around comes around. The ball is now in your court, so I need leave you to decide. (She stood up and went to bed).

What a dilemma! I felt confused and disturbed. I stood up and started blaming myself while wandering in the room for lack of self control. Had it been I have not slept with Amanda now, it would have been easy for me to back out. While on my thought, I heard my phone ringing...

I looked at the screen and it was Amanda, then I picked the call...

Amanda: Hello dear, hope you were not disturbed by the rain?

Me: Not at all

Amanda: you left your wrist watch in my room.

Me: oh! It was true. Just keep it for me.

Amanda: alright dear. When are you coming for it?

Me: I can't say for now, perhaps weekend.

Amanda: that will be better then, because myself wanna see you that very weekend. I have a very crucial issue to discuss with you.

Me: can't we just discuss it on phone now?

Amanda: is not a matter we could discuss on phone. It has something to do with you, Louisa and myself.

On hearing that, I was shocked and I started sweating despite the fact that it was raining

Me: I am scared. Wait Amanda, can we see tomorrow please? (I asked out of tension)

Amanda: you know the nature of my work now, and you will also be at work tomorrow. I think the best day for us is weekend.

Me: tomorrow will be my last day at that office, and I am only going there to sign my logbook. Therefore, no problem on my own part.

Amanda: that's interesting! So, you won't tell me if not because of what we are discussing now?

Me: I am sorry for that. I had the intention of telling you when I came to your house, but it escaped my memory.

Amanda: no problem. Though, I will be available at night, but I am not in support of you visiting at night.

Me: I don't like it as well.

Amanda: then, you will have to wait till weekend. May God spare our lives.

Me: Amen.

Amanda: splendid night rest. Love you wholeheartedly.

Me: love you too. Take care of you.

Amanda: I will. Thanks so much. Bye…(she hung up the call)

I threw my phone on the chair, and then stood at akimbo looking sad, sober and depressed like a player who lost a penalty kick at the final.

I later composed myself and got over the pressure.

It was weekend, Saturday morning when I received a call from Louisa…

Louisa: hello dear, how was your night?

Me: it was fine and yours?

Louisa: Glory be to God.

It was funny to me because I was hearing such from her for the first time.

Me: Louisa! Did you just say 'Glory be to God's?

Louisa: (cut in) what do you mean? I'm now a practicing Muslim, in fact if you see me, you will glorify Allah.

Me: (happy) really?

Louisa: yes. You know what?

Me: I don't know, until you tell me.

Louisa: I'm currently in State, but I don't know how to get to your house, so I need your address.

Me: (exited) are you serious? I can't just believe this! So, I'm still gonna see you again? Ooh! I feel good, (playing guitar sound with month)!

Louisa: laughing....

Me: just wait, let me quickly get a bike, I am gonna join you in the next ten minutes.

Louisa: I am coming with a car. Just send me the address and I will get to you.

Me: really? a moment please.

I dropped the call and quickly sent her the address within a tick and then called her back...

Me: have you seen it?

Louisa: yes. Am gonna join you very soon.

She dropped the call while I quickly arranged my room. I informed my sister about her visit and pleaded to her (sister) not to shun her which she conformed.

After ten minutes, I received a call from her...

Hello dear, I'm at St. David High School School, but one my tyre is flat and I don't know how to fix the extra Tyre.

Me: I am gonna join you now.

I dropped the call and jumped out of the room. I got to the place within short period of time.

I can't just believe it was Louisa, she appeared in a sumptuous navy blue overall and hijab coupled with spectacle on her face. I was so impressed and enticed with her new look. We exchanged pleasantries. After that, I asked for the jerk and the extra tyre which she provided without any time wasted. I bent down jerking the car when one Honda accord car parked beside us and three thugs came out of the car together with Amanda.

We were shocked and started wondering...

"Amanda, what's all this?" Louisa asked to break the silence and a hot slap landed across her face from one of the thugs.

"Good! This idiot (pointing at Louisa) is trying to play upon my intelligence. Next time when you come to this world, you will know the kind of person you play dirty games with. Carry that man into the car and kill the idiot", Amanda ordered the thugs to arrest me. I tried my best to set myself free while Louisa was crying bitterly, but all the effort went in vain. They locked me up in the car and one of them brought out a pistol pointing to Louisa...

"Say bye bye to this world and to this gentle man", the thug said with deep voice and before we know it, gunshot was heard...

I shouted, "no o o o" when I felt down from the chair and my sister rushed out from her room, "Kyle! Kyle! What happened? What's the problem?" she asked out of worried while I was panting heavily like someone who just completed a marathon race. I wiped my face to be assured that it was a dream and yes it was.

"Ah! It was a nightmare (still panting)", I replied her.

She placed her left hand on her chest while the right one was wrapped across my neck and relaxed by tilting her head towards my left shoulder, "take care dear", she said with care. And gradually, I came back to my sense. Then my sister went back to her room. It was still rain raining, I looked at the wall clock and it was around 10:55pm. I stood up and observed my prayer before I went to bed. I got over my troubled mind when the rain stopped finally and slept off after some minutes.

I woke up late the following day which way Monday. I observed my prayer and prepared for work after some minutes. I did not rush because the day happened to be my send-off. I got to my place of work to see the office decorated. I was surprised thinking there was a program on that day, until when my Bosses started singing the farewell songs for me. They started this when my phone started ringing. I looked at it and when I discovered that it was Louisa, I quickly switched it off so that she would not use her reggae to spoil my blues. I was commended and complimented with gifts for my hardworking, commitment to work and loyalty. We took pictures together and my logbook was signed and stamped for me. In fact, it was really colourful.

I left the office happily and returned home.

I was a bit tired because of the fun I had at the office, so I decided to rest. I woke up around 5:52pm and decided to switch on my phone, then a message entered from Louisa and I read, "the moments of loneliness without you were like enslaving me in love, these are the time I came to realize how precious you are to my joy. I miss you so much that I did not hear from you. You mean a lot to me, in fact, you are a rare gem. Let my trust continue to be in you. Love you to the bone. Beep me whenever you are available".

I was emotionally touched with her message. "Definitely, Louisa is still very much interested in me, but how do I go about Amanda's issue?" I soliloquized. Then, I put a call to her, but her number was not reachable.

When it was around 7:45pm that very day, I got a call from Amanda...

Amanda: Hello, how are you?

Me: I'm fine, and you?

Amanda: I'm doing well too. So, how was the logbook? Has it been signed for you?

Me: Yeah. In fact, they really made it a colourful day for me. I was presented gifts, we danced and took pictures together, all sort of things.

Amanda: That's lovely. That means I missed a lot.

Me: Not that much.

Amanda: ok.(moody) Kyle, I must confess to you that I am seriously in love with you and can't afford to lose you, but... (Stopped)

Me: But what?

Amanda: Don't worry. When we see, everything is gonna settle.

Me: But why now? Can't you just tell me something?

Amanda: I'm gonna uncover it, not something, but everything because my conscience is even disturbing me.

I was lost with what she just said.

Me: I can't get you; can you please shed light on what you just said now?

Amanda: later. Goodnight. (She hung up).

I started wallowing in confusion and could not't just think straight but soliloquizing.

I got a call from her (Amanda) on Wednesday around 6:00pm telling me that she was free and I should join her if I could make it. I left home without hesitation and got a bike to her house...

It took me like ten minutes to get to her house. We exchanged pleasantries and offered me a sit which I did without hesitation. We sat facing each other. She felt cozy on her seat looking moody.

"Sometimes, there exist something to discuss, but there will be no time. Thank God that we have what to discuss, and we have gotten the chance of discussing it", she said and continued, "I have to tell you this, so as to set my conscience free, and at the same time to open your eyes because you are in darkness. You must have been wondering why I got hooked to you despite the fact that I did not know much about you. I want you to erase the thought now because I know much about you. I want us to resolve this issue before Louisa's arrival which is the end of this month (this coming Sunday)"

I was shocked when I heard this and could not utter a word. I wished to say something, but words just did not come out.

She continued, "I don't want to be an ingrate and I don't want to bite the finger that feeds me", she stood up and started wandering in the room while she continued talking, " Louisa and I were childhood friends and even family friends because her dad and my dad were business partner. Some years back, we were in the sitting room when hoodlums visited our house. They killed my parents, raped me which made me lost my virginity and also lost my twin sister just because he proved manly to them", she kept sweating and tears were rolling down her cheeks while my mouth was widely opened and my lips were relaxed.

She continued, "Louisa's father was the one who came to my aid, financed my studies by sending me out of the country and Louisa later joined me after she aborted for you. She explained everything that transpired between both of you to me and how much she loves you because you are trustworthy. She showed me the pictures you took together when you were in polytechnic. I have phobia for guys as a result of my experience too, but owning to the way you were being presented to me by Louisa, the phobia disappeared and I started having interest in you. Louisa's father was the one who got me the job in the bank. The first day I saw you in the bank, I was shocked because I never thought we could meet. Though, I was not so sure very well that it was you, but I informed Louisa that I saw you. And I told her that you looked charming and that you must be a womanizer. She asked me to seduce you to confirm if you are still trustworthy and still in need of her so that she would prepare for wedding with you. If you could remember vividly that she called you the following day you came to the bank, I was the one who gave out your number to her and she was the one who asked me to send that one thousand dollar to you. I was the one who told her to shift her coming day to end of the month that I will need little time to carry out her assignment. I did not disclose to her that something has happened between us instead I told her that you still remain the man she knows.

Now, the ball is in your court to play. What is the way out?" she confessed bitterly with her top soaked with sweat coupled with tears.

I took a deep breath. I felt sad and sober. I was short of words and did not know what to say…

After some minutes of deep silence, I summoned courage and spoke out…

"Amanda, sit down", I commanded her and she sat reluctantly. I sighed before I started talking again

"In fact, I really appreciate and commend your effort for taking your time to shed light on this issue and at the same time share from your feelings and sympathize on that of your family. This issue is a serious task for me to handle all alone. We both have to deliberate and decide on it. To be sincere, I have created feelings for you, but sequel to the explanation you gave which I also reason along with, it will be very bad of you to do such to her and her family. In fact, it does not speak well, but how do we go about that?" I stylishly put the question to her.

"Though, I still love you, but we just have to cut the love to save both of us. We have to let bygones be bygones and leak the secret not to her. That's my own suggestion", she said while tears started rolling down her cheeks again. I drew her closer towards me and hugged her tightly while I was trying to fight back the tears rolling down my cheeks as well.

We left each other and stared at each other for a moment. I felt sorry for her which increased my feelings for her. I closed my eyes, sat back and tilted my head to the back when I felt a warm kiss on my lips. I responded immediately and our lips started fighting the war of supremacy again. Suddenly, I resisted and withdrew myself, "Amanda, I have to leave. Remember, we have to stop this!" I said and stood up. She looked at me with passion and kept mute. I knew she wanted to say something but she has to keep mute.

"Get me the wrist watch. It's high time I left because it is already dark", I said when she went in sluggishly and came back with the watch. She saw me off out of the house and waited with me till when I got a bike to my area. Her eyes followed me till she lost sight of me while waving to me as if we are not going to meet again.

She called me when I got home to ask about my movement. In fact, she was really loving and caring.

"Louisa was really the architect of this problem. Why must she test monkey with banana? She has to be blamed for whatsoever that comes out of this", I taught to myself

I had a sleepless night that very night as I was just pounding on what could be the end result of our game.

My sister asked about the latest development but I refused to reveal what has happened to her because I knew she would discourage me more. I received calls from both of them from that day till Sunday when Louisa finally came around...

She called me around 6:00pm on that very day telling me she was around and eager to see me...

Louisa: I'm now in State. In fact, I can't wait to see you.

Me: Good to hear this. How was your journey? Hope it was not stressful?

Louisa: It was, but thank God. How do I get to you?

Me: My side is difficult to locate. Perhaps you tell me where you stay so that I can join you and we can as well come back to my side together if time permits.

Louisa: Alright dear, that would be the best. I'm gonna text you the address when I hang up the call now.

Me: Alright.

Louisa: Love you so much.

Me: Love you too.

She dropped the call and sent me the address via text message. When I checked the address, it happened to be same address as that of Amanda.

"Oops! How do I go about this? Amanda and Louisa in a house! How do I react when I get there? What could be Amanda's reaction when I got there? What of if Amanda has betrayed me by leaking the secret to Louisa? Or these ladies are trying to play me?"

Those were the questions running through my mind with no response. I felt remorse for my action with Amanda.

After some minutes, I cheered up and prepared for the worst. Though, I had taken my bath in the morning, but I still went to bathroom to shower and dressed up for her house. I told my sister that Louisa was around and possibly, we might come back together so that it would not meet her unprepared and I zoomed off to her house.

When I got there, I stood opposite the yellow bungalow house doing nothing but contemplating whether to go in or not. I stared at the window hoping to catch a glimpse of what was going on inside but saw nothing.

Although my instinct urged me to turn back while thinking about the questions that were begging for the answers which I have asked myself, but yet, I belled the cat. I punched the door bell with a finger and it rang melodiously when it felt my touch. I waited for a reply but I did not hear one until the second time when a feminine voice spoke from the inside.

A few minutes later, when the door was opened, I was stunned by the sight I behold, the figure standing before me was that beautiful damsel with an extravagance attire. Her charming smile was so sumptuous. The surprise on her face was enormous when she saw me; she jumped squarely on me with her lips finding mine...

"I missed you so much baby" She intoned, stealing more kisses.

"I missed you more", I replied apathetically sequel to the wound she has created in my heart through the test she conducted for me which I failed.

We looked at each other in a special way; in fact, I did not know how to describe her beauty. She dragged me in while my heart was pounding heavily.

I sat down and put on a fake smile while she was trying to get me what to entertain me...

"Louisa", I called.

"Yes dear", she replied.

"Come over, we need to talk", I said.

"Alright dear", she replied and came around.

I commanded her to sit down which she did immediately with joy. She started staring at me with passion.

"Please, what is going on here? Because I'm confused" I asked.

She smiled...

"What are you confused about?" she replied comfortably.

"I have once been to this house when I was invited by a friend I told you last time, but which I ran away when she was trying to seduce me", I said.

" It was true. I thought you would fall into my trap, but fortunately for you, you passed the exam", she said joyfully.

What! What were you insinuating? Why must you test me through her? Assuming I was a womanizer, what do you think would have happened? So, you could still doubt my feelings for you? Oh my God! I said accusingly and burst into tears.

She quickly stood up from her sit and started begging me while she was on her knees...

"I'm sorry dear, we were joking with it before it turned to real, and again, I did that just because I have my trust in you and can boast of it anywhere. I know I made mistake, but please, forgive and forget about it", she said regrettably while weeping bitterly.

I hugged her tightly and from there, we started kissing...

Our tongues started fighting the war of supremacy as we twisted, entwined and entangled it in action. In fact, her action showed that it has been long she has done it. She needed it badly which I was also ready to offer her, but unfortunately, Amanda came around which made us shocked and quickly separated immediately. She looked at us with hatred, hissed and went in. We felt embarrassed...

"Could you see what you have caused now", I said accusingly.

"I'm very sorry dear. I'm gonna talk to her", she pleaded.

"That will be better, otherwise I will stop this relationship with you because I will not like to be in a relationship where my life will be at stake", I threatened.

"I'm gonna work things out. Just give me little time to work on it please. I'm seriously sorry for any inconvenience this might brought to you. I highly regret it", she said soberly and went in with Amanda. She came back after some minutes with Amanda smiling.

"I'm very sorry for all what I have done to you. Hope you would be so glad to forgive and forget about everything?" Amanda requested.

I stood up from where I sat and hugged her and said, "Bygones are Bygones".

Louisa seemed like the happiest person on the earth at that very moment. She clapped her hands and shouted "hurray! She rushed in and came out with a bottle of non alcoholic wine and three glasses. She poured the wine into the glasses and handed them to us. We clinked the glasses and had fun together that very night.

She presented various things like T-shirts, suit, shoes, trousers among others to me and Amanda assisted in carrying it to where I got bike when I was going. I basked in between them as if they were my entourage. I got home happily that very day and gist my sister when but did not let her know that Louisa was the source of the problem. Louisa called me when I got home and gave the phone to Amanda to speak with me as well. I was over joyous and felt on top of the world that very night. In fact, my night was also special.

The following day, I got a message from Louisa telling me to come over that Amanda has gone to work and she was feeling lonely. I took my bath and dressed up by putting on one of the wears she brought for me. My look was charming and inviting which could drive ladies crazy. I joined her in a short period of time. When I got there, what I saw her with was seriously killing and made me lost totally. The camisole top she had over her upper half was pink and it was dropping rather low giving me the deepest cleavage I've seen long. She put on neither skirt nor tight but g-string pant showing every trace that made up her roundedness providing the dotted outline of her puffy pussy. I was just standing like a log wood looking at her like a lizard without knowing what action to take. She stared at me and put on a sexy smile...

"Why are you looking as if this thing is strange to you? Am begging join me. I'm seriously in need of you, or you have turned to father?" she asked jokingly...

"Did I here you say father? See you, am gonna finish you today", I replied while moving closer to her.

She giggled and started running away from me while I ran after her. She felt on her bed in the room when I caught up with her and started playing with her. We started from kissing. We twisted, entwined and entangled in action. I slipped in a finger into her pant and gently dipped it into her honey pot, which instantly sent waves of current into her head, because it really had been quite long she felt a "manly touch" in that spot. I brought down my lips and kissed her again, this time more strongly than the old kisses. She closed her eyes, and moaned softly for me, which really got me excited......

I grasped her two bosoms and squeezed them softly, while her heart, body, and soul opened up for me

"Oh it has been quite long I felt a rod slide into me", she muttered to herself, as I allowed her caressing me. Her touches and caresses that time around were so special. I thrust in again and again, while she dug her fingers on my chest as I endured the pain silently, because she noticed I was enjoying it and so in order to make me happy, she let me have my way. I was so gentle that night as I expertly opened and penetrated deep inside her honey pot with my joystick and the smile on her face said it all as I moved my waist to and fro. She groaned softly which inspired me more. I tenderly kissed her, as I fondled and caressed her innocent looking bosoms and I knew not how I felt that moment, because it was a mixture of pain and pleasure. I slowly increased the tempo of my thrust, which also left me gasping for breath as my joystick penetrated and opened her kitty more and more which made her moaned loudly, "Please stop it's okay" she finally pleaded as she strongly held me, while I gazed into her eyes and jerked as if something had pushed me from behind, before lying on top of her.

She closed her eyes as we both breathed deeply and gently. We both stood up after some minutes and went to bathroom to have our bath. We wined and dined together before we zoomed off to my house. I introduced her to my sister and she did well to her. We discussed and caught fun. In fact, it was really a day.

She got a call from Amanda when it was around 7:05pm which made her left for that day.

The following day which was Tuesday, she came to my house where we planned about our future…

"I will be leaving for school next week God's willing", I said.

She stared and looked into my eyes with passion…

Louisa: I'm gonna miss you a lot.

Me: I'm gonna miss you too.

Louisa: In fact, I feel like going with you if not for some pressing issue I'm attending to. Anyway, I'll be checking on you in school whenever I feel like seeing you. Therefore, you have to be expecting me at anytime.

Me: That's lovely. You are always welcome. But wait, how do we go about your dad's issue with me?

Louisa: There will be no problem whenever we are ready for the introduction and wedding. Just leave that to me, I'll handle it perfectly.

Me: Are you sure?

Louisa: Trust me dear.

I was happy and hugged her, "love you so much dear", I said while she reciprocated it back.

Louisa: So, what are the arrangements you have put in place for the resumption?

Me: Nothing much on ground for now, but I trust God.

Louisa: All is well dear.

Me: Amen.

We played and had fun together. I heard her phone ringing when it was around 6:45pm and when I checked who was calling, it happened to be Amanda but I did not pick it for her and thereafter, my phone started ringing and it was same Amanda. Then, I picked it up without hesitation...

"Hello dear, how are you doing?" she asked with caring manner.

"I'm very much ok. How was work?" I replied and asked.

"It was fine. I'm now at home and feel like seeing someone like you beside me. I have really missed you. Wait, is Louisa not with you?" she asked curiously.

"She is with me, but currently in the toilet", I replied.

"All is well. Just help tell her I am waiting for her at home" she said and hung up the call without any good bye message. I was hit by her last words and reaction. "What has gone over this girl again?" I murmured to myself while Louisa came back.

She can see I was disturbed, because it was written on my face and asked about what has happened which I told her nothing...

"You have gotten a missed call from Amanda" I said.

"Now, I understand", she said and picked up her phone trying to put call to Amanda when I interrupted "what did you mean by your word", I asked anxiously and by then, she has started chatting with her. I stared at her till when she was through with the call and repeat the question.

"I am very sure that Amanda has called you, or did not she?" she asked curiously.

"Yes, she did" I replied immediately.

"To be sincere, I really don't know what's wrong with her; even she has changed to me at home. I know I'm responsible for whatever action she has embarked on to hurt you. I'm very sorry" she confessed and pleaded to me.

"Forget about that dear. It's just a normal thing and there is nothing new under the sun. It's only that you will need to take things easy and as well be careful with her", I replied.

"Thanks a lot sweetie" she appreciated and offered me a peck. She later left for house that very day. When it was on Saturday, I decided to pay her an impromptu visit which I never thought it could bring disaster, but unfortunately, I did not't meet her but met Amanda cooking. She attended to me very well. When I asked her about Louisa's movement...

"She got an urgent call from Dad and promised to be back tomorrow", she replied. I was worried and tried to put call to her, but her number did not go through. After some minutes, I heard my name from Amanda...

"Won't you come over and assist me, Kyle?" she said peeping through the elaborate shelf placed between the living room and the dining room. I was shocked to hear such from her. She was asking for my help for the first time. Why was the name called in a pet form? I thought before I answered "Sure, I will" and then joined her in the kitchen washing plates. "Please scratch my back for me" she pleaded.

" I stared at her and she gave an excuse "my hands are soapy". I knew her hands were soapy but I doubted this was going to be as normal as the world would want it. "Com'on Kyle", I heard her pleaded again. I just have to be of help, so I came closer and stretched my right hand while standing beside her and began to scratch her back through the fabric of her tank top. She made movements with her back in a bid to bring the appropriate place to my attention of which I tried reacting to accordingly. However this continued longer than I expected and soon she was saying I was not scratching the right place. I had to ask her to say where exactly she wanted me to scratch.

"Towards my hip" was the reply I got. "Hip?" I muttered inaudibly. Thought she said her back earlier? How come we are traveling down now? I felt the stir below and my joystick began gaining steel strength slightly. As I did so, she asked me to go further down. This means I should literally get hold of the band of her shorts. However, I went further down, purposely lifting her tank top a bit and exposing the skin of her back. "Go down further. It seems it's traveling down" she had stopped washing but just held one hand with the other while resting her elbows on her knees. I could smell the heightened sexual tension between us in the air and I swear I smelled her scent. She was wet!! I lost control again and my hand travelled down her ass globes. We both knew I had stopped scratching centuries ago and was now completely caressing her. But she wanted it taken further down as she feels it traveling. I had no idea what was making the journey.

I gripped her left ass cheek and gave it a real grab. She was now very turned on! I could easily smell her juices! So musky and intoxicating. The sheer material of her shorts made it almost easy to feel her wetness. I gradually travelled to her crack and freed my second hand to grab the other cheek. I was running crazy. She was just giving out slight moans while attempting to grind her hips into my grip. We were both enjoying this and only had one prayer; Louisa. I was now standing directly behind her. I changed tactics and through the legs of her shorts, slide both my hands into the nakedness of her two globes. She gave a quick gasp and tried raising herself a bit but I held unto her naked buttocks. They were so fucking soft and I endlessly played with them. Her juices were running like fresh water from rocks as they met my knuckles which reminded me that she has got a pussy too. I gladly directed both my thumbs to them and easily slide them into hers. Oh mine!! She groaned loudly. It felt so slippery in there and I soon got lost in a blur of constant movements in and out the honey pot with both my thumbs. She was almost audibly screaming and at a particular point had to call out my name loudly as I felt her g-spot while directing them below. It was now too much to bear so I had to counter the sensation that had made my joystick swell so much to the point that it hurts. We both had found a rhythm now. I had about three fingers buried in her pussy through the legs of her shorts that had travelled unevenly up into her hip while she endlessly ground and crushed her hip against those fingers. I was in turn stroking my joystick through the material of my shorts and even though I expected her to assist me, but she did not bother to make the plea. She was burning like wild fire. She had almost made it up now and had her left arm crossed over my neck while I gave her support by standing directly behind her. "Oh Kyle" she purred. This drove me further the edge and I quickly released myself from her tangle, dropped low and pulled her shorts towards her thighs. She quickly held unto it half way down her round buttocks; she was conscious of Louisa I guess; even though I could still clearly see her puffy pussy lips. They were so swollen and dark. I was staring at it when we heard the door bell ringing...

On hearing that, we quickly clad ourselves and started running helter skelter in a confused manner. I quickly rushed back to the sitting room and sat down with my one leg crossed over the other pretending as if I've been waiting for her arrival while Amanda quickly rushed out to the gate. She hissed when she came back. "What was the issue? Where is she?" I questioned anxiously.

"Don't mind that man that just used his own reggae to spoil my blues. He wanna lend something. Idiot!", she said angrily with her eyes coloured.

"Thank God it was not her", I said when she replied immediately "if it was Louisa? What will happen? Will heaven fall? Of course No! So, forget about that and let's enjoy ourselves before her arrival". I was shocked to hear such from her again since she was the one who suggested the solution. I was just looking at her with my mouth wide opened. Then, she moved closer to me and started caressing me which got me lost again. My joystick started gaining strength and when she was on her action, my phone started ringing beside me, Louisa calling, she quickly took my phone and off it. The action got me annoyed which made me yelled at her, "what's all this rubbish?" I questioned angrily and she was shocked and scared when she saw my eyes turned red. I pushed her away, picked my phone and left the house...

When I got back to my house, I tried to put call to Louisa but her number did not go through, it was switched off. I dropped my phone on the bed and I started packing what to take to school into my bag. Then, I heard my phone ringing, Amanda calling, I neglected all her calls while she later sent me a text message which I read thus; "it pains a lot when you see someone you love loving someone else and maltreats you because of that person. It creates wound in someone's heart which could devastate her life. What you have done today has shown me who you are and I promised you won't go free. You gonna pay for your action. Just try to mark my words"

I was shocked to receive such message from her. What did she mean? Was she trying to threaten me or what? Good to have this message on ma phone as an evidence. It's high time I leaked the secret between us to Louisa" I said to myself. Then, I re-dialed Louisa's number but still off. My system changed and could not concentrate on anything. I was thinking whether to call Amanda and reply her, but I controlled my anger and buried it. I completed the day in moody status. The following day, around 12:00 noon, I received a call from someone through Louisa's number which got me scared...

I picked up without hesitation…

"hello, is this Kyle on the line please?"

"yes, I am Kyle. Who's this please?" I replied in an effort to know the voice, when he spoke out again.

"This is Dr. Bello from State hospital, United State. The owner of this number got involved in a fatal car accident and she has been brought here, so your urgent attention is needed", he muttered and hung up the call. His last word hit me hard! I was shocked and almost collapsed at what he just disclosed.

My mood was destabilized and I did not know the next line of action to take…

"Could it be that Amanda has started her evil work? How do I get her Dad informed? Should I go to the hospital now or I should find a way of getting her informed first?" those were the questions begging for answers in my mind. I summoned courage and put call to Amanda, but she refused to pick up and that was when I decided to go to the hospital myself. I did not bother to take my bath; I just took a cloth from the wardrobe and rushed out without letting my sister know anything about it. I was about to enter the hospital when an ambulance with active siren speeded out from the hospital through the entrance. I quickly rushed into the hospital and called the number. I was almost slumped when the doctor told me that "her case was critical because she sustained severe head injury and therefore, she has been transferred to another hospital" I stood at akimbo for some minutes while my cloth became wet with sweat immediately. The doctor made it known to me that her dad has been involved and he was even trying to fly her out of the country. "What a sad and pathetic situation! is not it that my last nightmare has started coming to reality? Why are these happening? Urgent action has to be taking", I soliloquized and then, I left the hospital and went home moody. I explained the ugly situation to my sister which she also pity and sympathized with me. When it was around 7:00pm that very day, I got a called from Amanda...

Amanda: Hello, I missed your calls in the afternoon.

Me: yeah. Did you hear from Louisa?

Amanda: Not at all, though she promised to come back today and I've even tried her number this evening but did not't go through.

Me: And you did not call daddy to ask about her?

Louisa: This is not her first time of doing such, so calling dad is immaterial.

Me: So, you did not hear that Louisa was involved in an accident? Is that where and how you wanna start your plan you threatened me about? So, killing her is the solution to the matter?

Amanda: (cut in) I beg your pardon! What do you mean? Stop alleging me of what I know nothing about please. And besides, which Louisa were you referring to?

Me: How many Louisa do you know?

Amanda: How possible is that? Louisa? Accident? Never. Please, am gonna call you back.

She hung up the call while I was wallowing in an emotional pain. I expected her to call back but did not see her brake light throughout the night. I lost appetite and my night was odd. The following day, I decided to call Amanda in other to ask about Louisa's health status...

She picked it up and started crying immediately which got me scared…

Me: What is the issue? How far about her health? I waited for her for some seconds to say something but she did not't utter a word, she was only weeping instead which got me annoyed.

Me: talk now! (I yelled).

I dropped the call with anger when I could not hear anything from her than crying. I got confused more because I could not reason and understand Amanda's reaction.

"Is it that Louisa is dead or why was she crying? No, she must not die! Never! She is too young to die. God, where is your face? Why am I passing through all this? Come to my aid" I cried bitterly and I was petted by my sister. We were expected to resume back to school that very week but due to the situation on ground, I could not and all my efforts to get in touch with Louisa were futile.

After some days, Amanda called and told me that she had been flied out of country…

Me: How can I get her father's number?

Amanda: He is out of the country as well, so you can't reach him for now except if he calls you.

Me: I know you will not give the number to me and that is unfair, but Amanda, what has she done for you to deserve that? The ingrate you claimed you did not wanna be then, is now what you have turned to. Are you trying to punish me through her or what? Because, I don't understand.

Amanda: (crying) my threat was just an empty one now. Can't you just trust me that I could not do such? You are my family and you are the ones keeping me alive, so how would you think killing or wounding you guys would be the best for me? What would I gain from that? It was just a coincidence and that my utterances were out of anger. Please and please, stop alleging me of what I know nothing about.

Me: (I sighed) I am not convinced with your actions and words. Don't worry, God shall expose and punish whoever is behind this issue. I said and dropped the call.

I tried to motivate myself and move on. I went back to school after two weeks and my school fees was sent to me by my sister a week after. Though, it was difficult for me to put away her feelings, but life must continue. I managed to write my industrial training report and also forced myself to read because I must not have any delay. I tried her number every successful day but never gone through, but I never for once tried that of Amanda because her action has made me created phobia for her...

After three months, my first semester exam was around the corner and I've started preparing to put in my best so as to come out with better result, I got a reggae call from Amanda which spoilt my blues...

"Hello, how far? Have you heard from her?" I asked anxiously. "No", she replied soberly.

Me: What about daddy, did you hear from him?

Amanda: Not at all. I even tried his number yesterday night, but did not go through and he did not call me too.

Me: All is well.

Amanda: Amen. (Trembling) I got an information for you...

Me: Good or bad?

Amanda: (she sighed), it depends on the window through which you view it, but to me, it's good. I'm not supposed to inform you about this, but I still have to tell you at the same time due to one reason.

Me: I'm listening!

Amanda: I threw up twice some days ago which prompted me to go for test thinking it was malaria but the result showed it that I'm three months pregnant.

Me: Preg what? Did I hear you say pregnant or what?

Amanda: Of course yes. Is it new to you or what?

Me: You must be joking. Perhaps, you go for another test because I have not done anything with you and besides, I'm not ready to settle down with you unless you find me Louisa.

Amanda: (raised voice) Listen and listen good Kyle, I'm not calling to trade words with you but just to get you informed and again, I'm not forcing you to bring anything but to know that very soon, you are gonna become a father. She lamented and hung up the call.

I was shocked and confused.

This lady with her problems all the time.

What should I do now? I was disturbed throughout that day. Though, it was difficult to do, but I later discarded and got over the problem, and then managed to write my first semester exam and left the school to our family house.

My room was dusty and there were hanging cobweb everywhere in the room. I could not stay long in the house because it was scary though, I tided up everywhere before I tried to locate James and thank God I found him.

We exchanged pleasantries by hugging each other and shared life experiences together where I told him about my problems with Louisa and Amanda... "friend, you are going to meet Louisa again but I will advise you to move on with Amanda pending the arrival of Louisa", he counseled.

I was confused with his words and seek for enlightenment...

"But what gave you the assurance that I'm still gonna meet Louisa again? And if you are very sure of that, why did you ask me to continue with Amanda since Louisa will be back?" I questioned anxiously.

He cleared his throat and replied, "Since Amanda claimed you have impregnated her, you will have to confirm her pregnancy and if it is true, there is nothing you can do to it than to accept. On Louisa's issue, since she was the architect of the problems, she must be ready to accept defeat and be the second wife if and only if she is ready to be. That's my own view", he concluded.

I took a deep breath as I reasoned along with his argument, but it's easy said than done. I appreciated him for his outstanding support. In fact, James was a friend indeed. We exchanged our new numbers before he took me out for fun. I stayed with him till the second day before I zoomed off to State where I also disclosed all what has happened to my sister. She blamed all of us for playing politics and alleged Amanda and I for betraying Louisa. She felt pathetic and shared from Louisa's feelings despite the fact that she was not there and advised me to move on as James counseled. Since, Amanda is always available throughout the weekend, then I decided to pay her august visit which got me shocked on getting there.

I could not't just believe she was truly pregnant. I wondered why her pregnancy was crystal clear even visible for the blinds to see. She was also shocked and flabbergasted to see me. She was confused and did not know whether to embrace me or run away. She just stood motionless with her mouth wide opened. I moved closer to her and hugged her tightly while she embraced me too and tears started rolling down her cheeks. I fought back the tears and we sat down. She stood again "just a moment please" she said and later came back with a bluish bottle of wine with a glass in a tray and put it on a stool in front of me... "Thanks for that, but I will not be able to take anything. I only came here to check on you and know about your welfare" I said in a weak tone.

"Thanks for that, but why are you taking nothing? Are you still not happy with me?" she replied like a beggar looking for Samaritan.

"I must be frank with you, I am not happy with what is going on and my conscience has not been allowing me to sleep.

Assuming Louisa came around now, what are we gonna say? What do you think she would say? I want you yourself to think about it and put yourself in her shoes. If you were to be Louisa, what would you do?" I confessed and inquired.

She sighed; her head was bent down and buried it while her left hand was placed on her left thigh. She stood up after some minutes and started wandering in the room while soliloquizing...

"If I had known that this is what will happen, I would not have engaged myself in such dirty game in the first instance. It's a big slap on my face but I don't have any other alternative than to accept it the way it has happened since I can't abort. I've once made an attempt of aborting it, but I was told in the hospital that I was just fortunate to conceive because there is fibroid in my womb and my chance of getting another one if I abort this is zero. I'm not happy about this too. In fact, I felt like joining my family because I'm tired of my life. I'm ashamed of my stupidity. Kyle, what do you think is the way out?" she confessed sadly and busted into tears.

I was short of words. What a dilemma! I stood up after some minutes and petted her to take heart...

"You mistakenly cut your fingers with knife and then threw away the knife, what has happened has happened. We were all at fault and guilty of our acts and there is nothing we can do than to accept our faith and learn from our mistakes. Take heart dear, everything is gonna be okay. I'm very much ready not to let you down, to be responsible for the pregnancy, to stand beside you and also ready to bear whatever risk that comes out of this even when Louisa comes around", I said calmly while she hugged me so tight...

"love you so much", she appreciated with tears tricking down her cheeks. We both accepted our destiny and decided to move on till when we hear from Louisa...

I introduced her to my sister who gave her some word of advice and encouraged her not to give up on the condition she found herself. The counsel brought her back to life and rekindled her lost hope.

I paid her regular visit to play and chat with her before I left back for school after three weeks of vacation. Her love started increasing day by day in my heart but yet, I could not let go two days without dialing my first love's number which was always not going through. The life that was once like hell was then getting lovely and cozy and my relationship with Amanda was then becoming perfect which made me concentrated on my studies without any problem. Elders say a child that knows how to wash hands will surely eat with elder. My generous attitude to her also made her increased in good deeds to me. What surprised me most about her was that she sent me cash whenever I was broke and least expected as if I informed her. It was always coincided.

******

To God be to glory, I completed my B.sc program and I was posted to serve at a state where I was fortunate to work with an Oil company. I was well paid and at the same time I did some kind of runs which yielded me more money. I sent money to my sister to get me a bungalow in preparation to settle down as a family man with Amanda which she did without any stress with the help of her husband who was an agent. I seldom visit home to check on my wife (Amanda) as a result of the distance but never let go of a day without hearing from her... Blood is thicker than water. May God bless my sister beyond her expectation because she really tried for both of us. In fact, I would have said she was my mother but since I did not't grow up to know how mother cares, then I would rather say she was my grandma because she stayed and care for her since I was not around.

******

One fateful night, I could remember vividly, it was Thursday around 1:45am when I got a call from my sister telling me that she was in a hospital and prayer was needed just because my wife was about to deliver and she had been carried to the labour room. On hearing that, my body system changed and I became restless. It was not less than fifty minutes when I heard my phone ring again, my sister calling. I picked it up without any delay… "Hello sister, has she put to bed?" I asked anxiously with tremble in my voice.

"I learnt that she can't put to bed herself and she needs to go through CS (caesarean section) and as a result of that, she has been moved to the theatre. Just keep your mind at rest and keep on praying. By God's grace, she will deliver safely and we shall hear from both the mother and the baby", she explained rendered words of encouragement.

"A a Amen" I responded with great fear in my voice and she hung up the call.

It was a big blow on my face and my heart started pounding heavily while I kept on repeating "CS" like a kindergarten student reciting 'A for Apple' along side with his or her teacher. I kept on moving up and down in the room for some minutes before I later picked up a kettle and performed ablution, and then started praying. After some minutes, I heard my phone ringing again which made me broke the prayer. And I was shocked and confused when I saw who was calling me…

It was Amanda, "how come? Has she given birth or what?" those were the questions dangling in my mind while I was still looking at the phone ringing till I lost the first call and finally picked it up when it started ringing for the second time.

"hello dear", I said stammering when she cut in "it's me Sarah Thank God, she has put to bed" she broke the news happily. " Ha! God, you are wonderful. You are indeed the greatest. You are worthy to be praised. Sister, wait, a boy or a girl?" I asked anxiously in exited mood.

"In fact, God is really great. Both, a boy and a girl (giggling)" she said joyfully.

I could not just believe what I heard, so I tried to confirm to be sure... "Please, can you just recap what you just said now? Do you mean twins?" I asked anxiously while I stretched my ears in an attempt to hear clearly. "Yes o o o, you are now a twin father", she re-affirmed her statement joyfully.

I praised God with surprise which means "God is great"... "I'm so happy to hear this good news. In fact, if anyone rides horse in my belly, he or she will ride smoothly without any hindrance. Thank you so much sister, I'm gonna join you as early as possible tomorrow, but may I speak with her?" I said joyfully and inquired.

"No for now, she is asleep" she replied.

"No problem then, later", I said.

"Alright , Kelly. Journey mercy in advance and take care of yourself", she replied excitedly and hung up the call...

I was so happy and felt like I was on top of the world and decided to spread the good news without minding that it was mid night. I put call to

James but he did not pick up which gave me an instinct to delay spreading the development to everyone who deserves to know about it till morning. I could not sleep till the dawn because I was just full of joy forgetting that there was a challenge before me...

The next morning, James called me back and I told him about the news which got him excited as well. When it was around 8:15am, I prepared for home but branched at office to get my boss informed and simultaneously took permission which he granted satisfactorily. I got home safely and checked on her at the hospital...

She was discharged after four days and people came from every nooks and crannies to greet her...

I thought I was dreaming when I saw Sophia who also came around to rejoice with us. I was shocked and confused, we stared at each other with horror face, then she made an irritating and elongated hiss which sent signal to everyone on seat and got them surprised, and then set eyes on her at a time. She stood up immediately,

"Amanda, I need to see you in camera. Would you join me outside?" she stepped out while our eyes followed her and Amanda followed...

After some minutes, Amanda came in with strain written all over her face and everyone on seat started looking at her with worried wondering what could have happened but could not't say anything.

"Where is Sophia that you followed?" I asked so as to emanate the non favorable situation on ground because most of them (well-wishers) were in darkness.

"She has gone, but promised to come back later", she replied in sour tone.

In the evening of that very day, I asked her about what Sophia told her but she did not't open up.

"Don't mind her. It was all about your past which I'm less concerned about. Though, I'm not happy but I have no option than to accept my fate", she responded while her eyes were saturated with tears.

Though, I was not satisfied with her stance and response but due to her present status, I needed to take things lightly with her which made me changed the topic to naming ceremony plan.

"Dear, what are the names you would like to give the babies", I asked with smile on my face while expecting her to reply in an excited mood but my expectation turned otherwise.

She looked into my eyes with sympathy and shook her head left and right, I was expecting her to say something, but nothing came out from her mouth. Her action got me scared, then I move closer to her and petted her

"Dear, what's the issue? What happened? This look is nothing to write home about, please, tell me something", I pleaded with strain all over my face. Then, the babies started crying which made my sister came around to assist her. She breastfed them but yet they refused to stop crying till around 3:05am. And around that time, I got a call from my boss telling me that my attention is needed and I needed to report as early as possible. I left my sister and wife very early in the morning.

I was about to enter the town when I saw a man in the pool of his own blood almost lifeless struggling to come out from a devastated jeep that ran into the bush. I felt care less about the incidence and drove off, but my mind could not just allow me to do so. Then, I stopped but did not kill the engine of my car and tried to rescue him. The driver has joined his fore-father, then I carried the man into my car not minding any implication that could come out of it and drove him to a nearby hospital in the town and he was urgently carried to A&E (Accident and Emergency) unit first and later transferred to ICU (Intensive Care Unit) just because he was unconscious.

I did the necessary things and my number was collected by the doctor in case of any assistance while road safety officials was called before I proceeded with my journey. I Joined my colleagues at work and when I asked of the boss, I was told that he just left the office as a result of a call he got, then I decided to move out and put call to him but he did not pick up...

Then, I decided to call my wife so as to know about her well being and that of my twins but she also refused to pick up which made me called my sister and the story was the same. I called both of them several times but no response. My mind was disturbed and I did not know what to do "these people are not matured enough to be using mobile phone, where have they kept their phones now?", I murmured.

I went back to the office where Ernest, a colleague at office challenged and delivered a message to me "where did you go before?" he asked inquisitively.

"Just to make calls", I replied.

"Alright, boss said you should work on this and submit the report before 6:00pm", he handed a file to me and winked me with smile written all over his face.

I collected the file from him and started the assignment immediately with no time wasted. Though, the work should not't have taken more than three hours but due to the pressure on me which made me spent additional two hours but yet, it was ready some minutes to 6:00pm and that was when my boss came around and the work was handed to him.

He went through it and said "in you I trust. Kudos for the work well done. How was your family at home? I would not't have disturbed you but just because you are the best to carry out this assignment for me. Next tomorrow is the naming ceremony right?"

"Yes sir." I replied and shook my head in affirmation with smile.

"Good! Be expecting me and my people" he said.

"Alright sir. Thanks a lot sir", I responded.

"You are free to go back home, the family man", he said in a jokingly and left the office and I replied "thank you sir."

Then, it was already past 6:00pm and I decided to call the mother of my kids again which I expected her to pick up but picked by my sister...

"Hello dear, where have you put...?", I was about to query her when she cut in, "it's me, your sister. Twins mother is not in good condition, she is bleeding and she has been taken to hospital. In fact, she is in a critical condition and she said she needs to see you. Therefore, you will have to show up as urgent as possible", she said with tremble in her voice.

On hearing this, I was shocked and felt sad...

"I will join you very soon", I replied in sad mood and dropped the call.

I quickly got the car key and started the car, I got to the hospital after six hours journey…

"Where is she?" I curiously asked my sister who lead me to the doctor's office and we went to her together…

I met her on bed looking very sick and started wondering what could have been the issue.

"Welcome dear", she said and she started struggling to get up in order to rest her back against the wall which I assisted her in achieving that.

I sat beside her while the doctor and my sister stood looking at her…

She looked into my eyes passionately and tears started trickling down her cheeks.

I wondered what brought about that and quickly wiped off the tears with my right palm.

"Dear, what's the issue? What happened?" I asked out of worried while the doctor stood looking at the drama.

She sighed and kept on staring at me passionately before she spoke out…

"I'm very sorry dear. I love you so much and care for you a lot, but it pains me a lot and wound has been created in my heart as a result of the medium through which we met and the silly mistake I made where I served as a stooge. Hope you will forgive me when you read through a letter I've written to you which I kept in the wardrobe? I'm gonna miss you a lot." she said and smiled while still looking into my eyes.

"Why all this dear? I also love you and care for you as well", I responded out of tension.

"Take care of my babies very well dear" she said and took the last breath…

I quickly held her and shook her vigorously calling her name Amanda, Amanda, Amanda while my sister started jumping up and down, "excuse me", the doctor said in an urgent tone. He quickly brought out a stethoscope and examined her. He shook his head left and right, looked at my face and that of my sister and then said, "I'm sorry, she is dead."

"Dea what? Doctor! How do you mean? Amanda! Amanda!! Please, just look at my face, please just answer me for a moment" I pleaded while shaking her but she refused to answer which made me busted in to tears while my sister was also rolling on the floor crying bitterly.

Amanda's body was covered with white cloth while we were dragged out of the room.

It was really a sad day for me. Arrangement was made for burial by contacting those that were concerned, but unfortunately for us, Amanda's guidance who happened to be Louisa's father was also in a hospital. It was confirmed that he had accident when he was coming home to check on Amanda who gave birth.

She was finally buried on the day that should be the naming ceremony through the help of my sister's husband who help spoke to the elders in Louisa's family.

******

I could not stay in my house but with my sister who was taking care of the twins.

Life became misery for me. I blamed myself for lack of self control "had I know, I would not have slept with her", I regretted my actions, "Kyle, why did you lose your sense of reasoning? You are endowed with knowledge, but you did not make use of what God has bestowed in you. You Impregnated Louisa and it landed you in trouble, were you supposed to indulge in such act again with that family?" I was soliloquizing while tears were tricking down my cheek and that was when my sister husband came around and consoled me to take heart…

******

Her death came as a shock to me which taught me a lesson that no one is too small or too old to die and this made me move more closer to God and asked for forgiveness for my shortcomings.

After three weeks, I was called at office to scan a document and send it through my email which forced me to go home. While looking for the document, I saw the letter written to me by late Amanda and I read through; "it is sadden that we won't leave together for long. I never thought it would be like this: if I had known, I would not have agreed with her: the stigma is too harsh and unbearable for me to endure; my conscience is disturbing me everyday for betraying someone like Louisa. Though, she has to be blamed as well but why did I accept to be a stooge? I think the only way to pay for my stupidity and also to let peace reign in your life and that of Louisa is to leave.

Don't be sad about my exit; remember, I promised to deliver my kids for you which I've done and the names you requested for from me to give the twins are here: the baby girl should be named Louisa while the boy should be named Kyle. I named them as such because I loved both of you (you and Louisa).

NOTE: You must marry Louisa and she must be the one to take care of my babies because I know you love each other and help me plead to her to forgive me because I have betrayed her trust in me and cheated on her.

You will have to forgive me too because Louisa asked me to drop you eighty thousand dollar into your account for your School fees and some other things needed before she left for th state to meet her dad. My ATM pin is 1212. I hope I've satisfied my conscience and I should be able to rest in peace.

Warning: don't marry any other person except Louisa and take care of my babies very well if you don't want trouble and you must not try to trace the cause of my exit...

Till when we meet where we shall depart no more. Amanda cares."

I read the letter with sadden heart and her words touched me. I felt guilty and pathetic for her exit and cried bitterly but later consoled myself when I thought of her last statement where she stressed that I must marry Louisa and also to take care of her baby if I did not want trouble. The question is where and how will I get Louisa who has disappeared for more than a year?

I took the letter to my sister and her husband when I could not reason on the way out and they were also shocked when they went through it and got the content of the letter.

Though, it was not that strange to my sister, but it got her husband lost which made him went crazy and lashed me with irritating words without minding my present status and that, I was also a father. My sister could not utter a word because she dare not say anything when the man is around while I bowed my head in acceptance of the defeat…

"You are not trustworthy and I'm totally disappointed in you. In fact, we have to leave you to dance to the beat of the trouble you have played" he said angrily and flung the letter while he left us on seat and worked briskly into his room.

I never expected such reaction from him and his reaction gave me the instinct of the strength and the intensity of the offence I committed…

******

I brushed my hair with my palm to and fro when my eyes were filled with tears and I nearly busted into tears which made my sister moved closer to pet me, "all is well dear. Don't worry, I will speak to him and justice will be done to it", she said and went in to join him…

I could not get myself right throughout that day not until the following day when the man called on me, sat me down and fed me with words of virtue and we later sketched out the plan on how to go about the issue…

My sister was asked to monitor the home while her husband and I went to the state in order to see Louisa's family. We called on James, who also informed his father about the scenario and we all went there together.

******

The elders that we consulted during Amanda's issue were met and they told us that only Louisa's father could tell us about Louisa and he was still in hospital and promised to keep us informed when he is alright. In fact, I could not just believe they could be lenient and so generous to us on such issue.

We appreciated them and left the place. James's father also gave us hope about the issue due to his relationship with Louisa's father.

The following week, I got a call from my boss to come but it was not urgent. I prepared for the journey and informed my sister. Though, her husband was not around, but I managed to put the call to him as well so as to get him informed about my movement.

******

When I was about to enter the town, then I remember that I carried a man to one hospital and my mind asked me to check on him to know about his welfare, but I rejected it and zoomed off to my destination.

My boss and colleagues sympathized with me on the issue of my wife and asked about the twins which I also thanked them for showing concern and for their supports through text messages and calls.

It was a great challenge for me to get over the issue most especially when I thought about Amanda's words in the letter and the emphasis she made on Louisa's issue. Assuming I was opportune to get in touch with Louisa, will she forgive me? If she does, what about her rigid father who has lost Amanda through me and almost lost his life in the process of checking on her? When I thought about those questions, my heart vibrated and I was tired of myself.

As day goes over day, I started getting over my troubled mind when I mixed with my people at work because they were all friendly and jovial.

I never let go of any day without putting calls to my sister and asked about how the kids doing.

******

One Saturday evening, around 9:15pm, I was in bed and about to sleep when I heard my phone ringing and when I looked at the screen, it happened to be a strange number which I pick without any delay…

"Hello o, who is this?" I curiously asked.

"This is Dr. Albert. Am I speaking with Mr. Kyle?" he asked calmly.

"You are very much on his line. Any problem?" I intoned without fear.

"Good! Thanks for the other day. In fact, more of your type are needed in our society. Here is the chief you saved his life and he is interested in speaking with you" he said (trying to handle the phone to the man)

******

"hello Mr. Man, how are you doing?" he intoned in big man voice.

"I'm very much okay sir. How is your body now sir?" I responded

"I'm now very much okay and I will be discharged probably tomorrow. Thanks so much. I really appreciate you and I will like to know you" He said and requested.

"I'm very happy to hear this sir. You are my father sir, and therefore command me which ever way you like it sir", I replied.

"You are blessed. That's my number, I will get you inform when I'm available. Thanks alot", he said.

"Alright sir", I replied and he hung up the call.

I was surprised to hear from him and at the same time happy to be the one whom God used to save his life. I quickly stored his number with "Chief" and later slept off.

I was expecting him to call me the second day

but I did not see his call. Then, I decided to follow the adages that says "if mountain refuses to go to

John, John should go to mountain" which made me put call to him but which he refused to pick up. On Tuesday of that very week, I got a call from James...

"Hello friend, you know what?" he curiously asked.

"I don't know, just tell me what happen", I replied anxiously.

"I pray nothing should happen, because

Louisa's father is now around and fainted when he heard about Amanda's death. He is now in my father's clinic and he has not recovered from the shock. Though, my dad should be able to know how to handle his case, but you still have to be very prayerful", he broke the intimidating news.

"Thanks for the information sir", I replied out of tension while my heart started pounding heavily and I did not know the next line of action to seek redress.

Then, I decided to inform my sister's husband who told me to keep calm, saying in as much the man lives and Louisa is also alive, there will be solution. He also asked me to join him at home on Saturday.

Sequel to the issue, I requested for permission from my boss to spare me the whole of the coming week which he granted without any stress.

I got home lately on Friday and branched at my sister's house, but her husband was not yet around.

I really pity my sister for the trouble I put her

into. Her beauty has faded and she has lost

weight due to the stress of the babies. I even wondered how she managed to cope.

My sister husband came around on Saturday and he told

me to prepare myself that we were going to the state on Sunday to sort things out. I put call to James to get him informed and he also told me that his

father is working on the issue by telling Louisa's father not to get mad at anybody due to his health status irrespective of what could have happened or what is happening ******

Coincidentally, my sister's husband got a call from an uncle to Louisa's father asking us to show up on Sunday which was our target day.

It was Sunday morning, we prepared ourselves

and called James to get set for the challenge ahead of us. That time around, my sister and her small boy Ope went with us likewise the twins.

On getting there, we met his uncles on seat and he was called upon to join us...

As he was coming down gently through the stairs case i kept on staring at him wondering if he was the one or not. "Could this be true? I don't think Its possible!" I kept on debating in my mind till when he finally be on a seat.

******

We exchanged pleasantries while he was staring at my sister but he did not utter a word. Then, my

sister's husband stood up and asked me to

prostrate while James also joined me… Louisa's father (Cut in) "please, I'm confused. Is this not James, my doctor's son?" he asked anxiously.

"Yes sir, it's me", James replied and put on a smile.

"What do you have for us?" Louisa's father

asked.

"It will be presented to you by daddy sir", he

replied gently while my sister's husband started the presentation…

Smith: I'm Mr.Smith, an uncle to Kyle whom your daughter, Amanda, (may her soul rest in perfect peace and may God take care of her children) delivered the twins to. May the

God Almighty in his infinite mercy give us

fortitude to bear the loss. We are really sorry for taking you to such bitter experience and all we have caused your family. Please, forgive us. We glorify God and give all adoration to him for sparing your life for us despite all the challenges you have gone through. We are very sorry once again. The issue on ground is seriously tough and

tedious for me to table, but I still have to say it

and please, I will really appreciate if you could

accept it which ever way I presented it…

In that course, a man from Louisa's family took over from him…

First uncle: Have your sit sir (he told my sister's husband) Thanks alot. We have told our brother

eighty percent of what you came here for and

everything has been settled, it's only that he needs to know the deceased's husband and how you will be taking care of her children because we are now in-laws and we need to take care of the twins together. Where is the twins father? He asked and that was when I stood up for recognition…

"Are you the husband", Louisa's father asked

anxiously while looking at my face and that of my sister interchangeably…

"Yes sir" I replied with tremble in my voice.

He paused for some minutes while he was staring at my sister, "twin mother, your face looks familiar to me. Have we met before?" he curiously asked while my sister nodded her head to affirm his question. "Where have we met" he questioned further.

"I was the one who came to you some years back as regards my grandmother issue who was arrested and later hanged to death" she replied and busted into tears while tears started tricking down my cheek as well. The whole room became silence as graveyard while Louisa's father was short of words. He looked at us with pity and then took a deep breath...

"What goes around always comes around, that is life. I'm very sorry for my harshness then. Please forgive and forget about the past" he pleaded while my sister nodded in affirmation and the man asked further, "hope this man (referring to me) was not the one who got my precious daughter impregnated then?"

I was shocked and my heart started beating very fast while those on seat kept on watching the drama he was acting.

"I'm very sorry sir" I uttered, which made him look at me with hatred and that was when an elderly man from his family stood up to talk. He cleared his throat and started "hun hun! You see, this issue is just like when mosquito perches on ones scrotum which needs alot of patience. If we refuse to forget about yesteryears saga, we won't get a friend to play with. In the light of this, I will want us to forget about the past issue and accept them as part of our family", he said which rendered Louisa's father sober.

Though, he was not totally satisfied, but he accepted and later embraced me...

******

"Thanks alot for these great opportunity you have given to us to be part of your family. We really appreciate it sir. But, is not over until it's over. We have a letter written by the deceased to her husband which also has something to do with the twins and Louisa. We will appreciate it alot if you could be of help on the issue sir", said Smith and I was instructed by Louisa's father to collect the letter for him which I did without any time wasted. He went through the letter and felt like crying while his family members on seat were wondering what could have made him reacted that way, he then gave it to them to go through it as well.

They were all short of words and started looking at one another.

Suddenly, the cry of the twins rented the air, which caught the attention of everyone and my sister quickly attended to them but they kept on crying which made Louisa's father stretched his hands so as to carry them. Everyone got astonished when they stopped crying. He was very happy and put on a smile...

"For the sake of these twins, I shall do justice to the letter. But the issue is just this, she should not be informed about Amanda's death because I can't afford to lose her", Louisa's father confessed.

When I discovered that Louisa's father has calmed down, then I used the opportunity to ask about her movement, "sir, is she back to the state?" I asked like a merciful being.

"No, she is abroad managing my business. Any problem?" he asked with no sign of anger which made me inquired further, no sir, only...

I paused because I was scared to say what was on my mind.

Everyone kept on looking at me...

"Young man, speak your mind, there will be no problem. Only that what?" Louisa's father intoned in a calm manner which made me gained confidence and spoke out.

"I received a call more than I year now from the state hospital through Louisa's number telling me that she was involved in a car accident and I later heard from Amanda that she was being flied out of country", I said while blinking my eyes like analogue clock.

He looked at me and smiled, "it must be a dream Mr. man and you should have woke up from your slumber immediately. God forbid! Nothing of such has happened to my one and only treasure and it will not happen while I'm still alive. I was the one who had accident and thank God I survive it" he responded without any reaction which got me confused. Then, many questions started bubbling in my mind, but my instinct told me to keep mute which I obeyed.

Then, the elderly man left his seat to discuss with Louisa's father in camera...

"We salute your courage for this giant step you have taken. In fact, you are very lucky because the person you are playing game with is not an easy type.

Sequel to your request as regards to the letter, you will have to give us little time to get In touch with Louisa and prepare her mind on the issue. We will contact you as soon as possible if and only if she is ready to take the responsibility", said the elderly man...

We thanked them and left the place with peace of mind.

A month after, I was in the office when I heard my phone ringing and when I looked at the screen it happened to be the chief which made me pick up without hesitation...

"Hello sir" I said happily.

Chief: How are you Mr.Kyle

Me: I'm fine sir. How about you sir?

Chief: I'm very much okay as well. Thanks for the other day. Hope you are not annoyed at me for just calling you since I've promised?

Me: Not at all sir.

Chief: I'm very sorry for that, it was just because I've been busy. So, where are you?

Me: I'm in the office where I'm serving.

Chief: That's good of you. So, you are still a corp member?

Me: Yes sir.

Chief: That's good of you! Hope you will not mind to be managing one of my companies when you are done with your service?

Me: (happy) I will highly appreciate it sir.

Chief: Good to hear that from you. When are we meeting in order to talk better?

Me: I will feed you back on that sir.

Chief: Alright dear, I would like to hear from you soonest. He said and hung up the call.

I was very happy to hear the good news from him and fed him back that I would be paying him the visit at the weekend, Saturday to be specific.

Though, I've once thought he should be the one while receiving his call but I later confirmed it when he described where he resides. It was same place where Louisa's father resides.

******

It was just like a dream when I got home on Friday and Smith told me that he just got a call from Louisa's father who told him that we should show up on Sunday of which I have promised him to be in his house on Saturday...

When it was Saturday, around 10:45am, I received a call from Louisa's father...

"Hello Mr. Kyle, how was your night?" he asked.

"I'm fine sir", I replied.

"When will you be around because my daughter is eager and interested in knowing you", he asked inquisitively.

"I'm on my way already sir", I replied.

"That's good! Journey mercy", he said while I replied with, "thank you sir" before he hung up the call.

"Louisa is now around", I said to myself. Then, I started experiencing mixed feeling of happiness and sadness and later got to my destination.

Louisa's father was shocked when he saw me, he looked at me with wonder...

"Why are you here today? You are to appear tomorrow, not today", he intoned in shock.

"I'm the Kyle you called some minutes ago sir", I replied.

"You!" he said pointing at me, "no, no, no, its not possible", he said while shaking his head left and right in disagreement and quickly dialled a number which rang in my pocket. He dropped the call and re-dailed the number and the same thing repeated itself. This made him got shocked and confused, "so, you were the one who saved my life?" He asked out of shock and I nodded my head in affirmation which made him dissolved into tears and embraced me.

We were on this drama when Louisa came out of a room and was shocked as well to see me. She did not know what to do neither did I know...

"Daddy, is this the Kyle you said he helped you?" she asked curiously.

"Yes dear", he replied with his eyes saturated with tears.

"Ooh no! I don't think it is possible! It should not be this wicked guy who has betrayed my love. Oh my God!" she confessed bitterly and busted into tears.

I felt sad and guilty of my action with Amanda. I made an attempt of petting her but she shouted at me, "if you dare touch me! You, the betrayal", she said out of anger, then she stood up and walked out on me which weakened me and made me looked helpless. I busted into tears which made Louisa's father spoke out...

"Be calm my son, you will have to go and come back tomorrow as speculated before, while I help you speak to her", he said and hugged me before I left the house.

It was really a big blow on my face. Though, I did not expect least from her, but I never thought she could go up to that length. After all, she was the architect of the whole issue.

I checked on James and updated him about the new development before I left for New York city and I also informed my sister and her husband about the scenario which got them shocked.

Though, the incidence was paradoxical, but they bought all what I told them and also gave hope to me by saying "the case has been settled since her father has promised to speak with her".

In the evening of that very day, I got a call from Louisa's father…

"Hello Kyle" he said.

"Yes sir", I replied.

"I'm very happy for you because she has promised to take the responsibility.Though, you all have to be blamed for the dirty game you have played but yet, you have to take the larger percentage of the blame due to your lack of self control. I believe this is how God has planned it and nothing could be done to dispose it. Therefore, we will be expecting you tomorrow for proper resolution of the issue", he confessed.

"Thank you a lot sir. I really appreciate your kindness and generosity. May the Almighty Allah in his infinite mercy be with you and your family sir. I have learnt my lesson in a hard way and therefore, I promise not to disappoint you. Thanks once again sir", I replied with grateful heart.

"It's a great pleasure for hearing such from you. We will be expecting you tomorrow", he said calmly.

"Alright sir", I replied and he then hung up the call.

My mind was filled with joy for the good news and I spread the gospel to my people who have been standing beside me through the hard time and they were all excited to hear.

I could not sleep well just because I did not know how I was feeling. I felt like hearing from her but her number did not go through...

Suddenly, I heard my phone ringing and it happened to be an unknown number which I was not scared to pick it up...

"Hello Kyle", she said and since her voice is unique to me, her name escaped from my mouth, "Louisa" while she giggled and then asked, "how did you know it's me?"

"Your voice is unique to me, even if I hear it while sleeping I will know it's you" I replied

"You and your sugar coated month. Thanks for that anyway. While are you not sleeping by now?" she asked inquisitively.

"I don't just know", I intoned soberly which sent her a signal and that was when I confirmed that ladies are feeble minded most especially when they are in love...

"I guess you are thinking over my reaction to you yesterday. I'm very sorry, I reacted in such manner out of anger because I was seriously hurt with what both of you did to me, but I later blamed myself for my mistake. I've forgiven you and ready to forget about the past and I hope you will do the same", she confessed.

"Forgiveness is divine. Thanks a lot for everything. I've forgiven you as well and I vow to be trustworthy to you", I replied soberly.

"Good to hear this from you", she said.

"Louisa, I have a question for you and will appreciate it if you could open up to me", I intoned gently.

"I promise to provide the right answer to what you wanted to ask me", she replied courageously.

"Thanks for that. I got a call through your number some years before now when I was told that you were involved in a car accident and I later heard that you were flied out of country for treatment. How true was that?" I asked.

She sighed and later spoke...

"I'm very sorry to have done that to you. It was not true. It was a planned work with the doctor that called you that very day. And the reason behind that was that a fortune teller told me to avoid you and leave this country if possible for like a year so as to avoid an untimely death and since prevention is better than cure, then I decided to subscribe to his warnings. I know I've gone wrong in some ways. Just forgive and forget for the sake of God and love", she confessed soberly.

I was short of words for some seconds before I later spoke out, "I've forgiven you", I said gently.

"Thanks so much dear. Love you so much", she replied joyfully.

"Love you too", I replied and she hung up the call...

My mind was at rest after the call and later slept off.

I took my bath very early in the next morning and prepared myself just because I was eager to see her. We later got there with my family and the case was settled.

Louisa's father and his family handed Louisa to me when Sophia came around which made my heart vibrated. She went on her knees in the presence of everyone and asked for forgiveness from both

Louisa and I for serving as obstacles which later resulted into Amanda's death.

Though, it pained but one just have to forgive and forget which we both did.

We appreciated everyone and left the place together with Louisa and she was trained by my sister how to take care of the babies and also became an expert.

After my service, Louisa's father fulfilled his promise by making me the managing director of one of his companies.

Louisa became a good mother by taking good care of the twins and she later had her own bouncing baby boy when the twins were two years of age and the all world graced the occasion and happily.